Teri Wilson is the author/creator of the Hallmark Channel Original Movies *Unmasking Mr Darcy*, *Marrying Mr Darcy*, *The Art of Us* and *Northern Lights of Christmas*, based on her book *Sleigh Bell Sweethearts*. She is a double finalist for the prestigious RITA Award for excellence in romantic fiction for her novels *The Princess Problem* and *Royally Wed*. In 2017, she served as a national judge for the Miss United States pageant in Orlando, Florida, and has since judged in the Miss America system.

Visit her at TeriWilson.net or on Twitter @TeriWilsonAuthr.

Besides, Ginny *chose* this life, just as surely as I chose mine. She also gets paid more for one sponsored Instagram post than I make in a week, and when I remember this, I keep my sympathy in check.

The elevator comes to a stop on the fifth floor, which has clearly been reserved for the pageant, because we all disembark in a glamorous, glittering herd.

Myself being the exception.

No one seems to notice my presence, though. The Hogwarts T-shirt I'm wearing might as well be an invisibility cloak. Fine. I'm not here to make friends. I'm here for the chance to stay in Ginny's luxury hotel room for a week, for *free*, and completely nerd out at the Wizarding World of Harry Potter.

I'm also here for moral support, of course. I plan on being at every single pageant event, cheering like a maniac while inwardly cringing in horror at the very thought of prancing around in only a tiny swimsuit and a crown. But since the competition doesn't start until 5:00 p.m., that leaves my mornings and afternoons free to hit up the theme park. I've emptied my paltry savings account and invested in a five-day unlimited pass. Bring on the butter beer.

But first, I must locate our room amid a sea of glitz and sparkle. According to the text Ginny sent when I landed, we're in 511. All of my elevator pals are in rooms along the same stretch of corridor. Half the doors on the floor have hangtags on the knobs that read, *Do not disturb! This Miss American Treasure contestant needs her beauty sleep!*

I roll my eyes mightily.

Dangling from the knob of room 511 is one such tag, but I highly doubt Ginny is actually sleeping because I can hear the television booming through the door. I knock extra hard so she can hear me above the din of whatever reality show she's probably watching.

Just please God don't let it be the Kardashians.

An explosion of barks answers my knock. I take a deep breath. I've somehow forgotten all about my sister's French bulldog mix, Buttercup. Ginny adopted her a month ago as part of her "platform." I'm not sure exactly what that means. She's a pageant queen, not a politician. But according to approximately five million posts on Ginny's Instagram, she volunteers regularly at her local shelter in support of her animal rescue policy.

If memory serves, last year her platform was anti-bullying. But so many other contestants on the pageant circuit had already thrown themselves into the anti-bullying movement that she felt pressured to switch to something else. In other words, she got bullied into giving up her anti-bullying platform. Oh, the irony.

The door to the hotel room swings open, and Ginny is standing there in a white spa bathrobe with her hair piled on top of her head in a messy-yet-artful twist. She's got one of those serum-soaked sheet masks stuck to her face—the kind that make regular people look like something straight out of a bad horror movie.

Except Ginny isn't a regular person. So instead she looks like Gwyneth Paltrow enjoying a quiet day of self-care.

"Charlotte, you're here!"

"Yep. My flight was right on time." Thank God. I'm ready to make the most out of day one on my unlimited pass.

"Come on in." She holds the door open wider.

The room is a double, with side-by-side queen beds and a balcony overlooking a pool flanked by umbrella-covered lounge chairs, a tiki bar, and two perfectly symmetrical rows of palm trees swaying in the balmy Florida breeze. Any spare moments I have this week that don't include Harry Potter will be spent right there, with my feet up and a piña colada in hand. It's been so long since I've taken an actual vacation that the mental picture I've just conjured nearly makes me weep.

"This is gorgeous. Ginny, thanks again for inviting me."

"Are you kidding? I'm so glad you're here. Dad and Susan aren't coming until the finals." Her smile falters. Behind the face mask, I can see her full lips tip into a frown.

I know exactly what she's thinking. "You'll make the finals. I know you will. You're a shoo-in for the top twenty."

Ginny always makes the finals. She's up onstage every

year alongside the winner and the runners-up. She's just never managed to crack the top five.

"This year will be different," I assure her.

She nods. "It has to be."

As much as I hate to see my sister devoting her life to chasing a silly crown, and even though I positively *loathe* the pageant scene, my heart gives a little tug. Sometimes I forget why she got started in all of this. But every once in a while, when Ginny's composure slips, I remember that this is her way of feeling connected to the mother we barely knew. The crushing sense of loss that inevitably follows always seems to catch me off guard. It's in those moments—moments like this one—that I understand her dream.

I paste a smile on my face. "It will. I promise."

I have no right to make that kind of promise. After all, I'm not judging this thing.

Truly, why would anyone want that job?

But it's so rare to see my sister like this that I can't stop myself. She's always been the poster child for confidence. Which just goes to show how much this particular pageant means to her. More than all the others combined.

"You're right." She nods with renewed vigor. "Of course I'll make the finals. This is my year."

"Definitely." Pep talk over for now, I head toward the bed on the far side of the room—the one that's still neatly made and not covered in anything bedazzled.

Every item on Ginny's bed shines like a disco ball, including her official Miss American Treasure tote bag. I'm beginning to understand why she uses one of those sleep-mask things like Audrey Hepburn in *Breakfast at Tiffany's*. I might need to invest in one myself.

As I cross the room, Buttercup launches herself at my wheeled suitcase, growling and nipping at it as it drags behind me. By the time I'm within a foot of my bed, she's fully attached herself to it and I'm hauling both luggage and bulldog.

"Is this normal behavior?" I ask. It can't be, can it?

Ginny waves a dismissive hand.

I give Buttercup a little nudge with the toe of my Adidas sneaker. She backs away, peering up at me with her bulgy little eyes. They almost seem to point in two different directions. Like plastic googly eyes.

We stare each other down for a second, and then she resumes her attack on my luggage.

"Is she always so"—I pause, struggling for an appropriate adjective—"headstrong?"

Buttercup and I have never been properly introduced. I only know her via Ginny's Instagram, where she's usually doing something less destructive and far more adorable.

"Buttercup is shy," Ginny says by way of explanation.

I look down at the snarling dog. "Sorry, I'm not getting shy here."

"You're stressing her out. She's not used to strangers and new experiences. She's a rescue dog, remember? The poor thing sat in the shelter for four months before I adopted her."

Ginny checks the position of her sheet mask in the large mirror over the bathroom counter. It's a double vanity, theoretically big enough for both of us. But Ginny's massive amount of toiletries take up the entire space. "Did you know that seven million dogs and cats enter shelters every year, and half of them end up being euthanized?"

I did *not* know that, and it's a horrible, horrible statistic. But her canned delivery prevents me from absorbing the news with the proper level of emotion.

She's slipped into pageant mode. She's rattling off more devastating facts and figures about homeless pets, all the while posing with her hand pressed to her heart and her head tilted just so.

I glance at Buttercup. Something tells me she's heard the speech before.

"Maybe less euthanasia talk in front of the rescue dog?" I suggest. No wonder the poor thing is stressed.

"Oh my God." Ginny blinks. "Do you think she understands?"

"I have no idea, but why take the chance?" Besides, I can't handle Ginny's platform-level intensity right now. I've been up since 4:00 a.m.

"I suppose you're right." Ginny scoops Buttercup into her arms.

I take advantage of the cease-fire, lift my suitcase onto the bed, and remove my things, paltry in comparison to the vast wardrobe Ginny has stuffed into the closet and all but one of the dresser drawers. Fortunately, I travel light.

Clotheswise, anyway. Beneath the layers of jeans and T-shirts, four hardback novels line the bottom of my bag. I remove all four and arrange them in a nice, neat stack atop the nightstand closest to my bed.

When I look up, Ginny's shaking her head. "Are you sure you brought enough reading material?"

"Don't judge. I'm on vacation, remember?"

"Exactly. You're a *librarian*. Your vacation should be book-free." Ginny makes a zero sign with one of her perfectly manicured hands.

"How are we even related?" It's not the first time I've asked that question, and I know with every fiber of my being that Ginny wonders the same thing sometimes.

How could she not?

"Before you dive into one of those, can you take Buttercup for a quick walk?" She grabs a Barbie-pink leash from her nightstand. And—*surprise!*—it's heavily bedazzled. "Pretty please."

"What? Why me?" My gaze flits toward Buttercup, who's now positioned on Ginny's pillow with her plump rear facing me. "She doesn't even like me. Stranger danger and all that."

Ginny rolls her eyes. "Stranger danger? You spend too much time with little kids."

True. She dragged me to yoga once, and I kept referring to easy pose as crisscross applesauce.

Still, Buttercup doesn't seem any more thrilled by the idea than I am. Also, I've already begun typing the address of the theme park into the Uber app on my phone. I'm supposed to be dodging a fire-breathing dragon in Diagon Alley right now, not walking a petulant French bulldog.

"I was kind of hoping to head over to Harry Potter World so I could be back in time for us to have an early dinner. Don't you have pageant stuff today?" I'm pretty sure she has a date with some spray tanner this afternoon. Her skin tone matches mine right now, and I know from experience that Ginny is usually at least four shades closer to orange when there's a pageant on the horizon.

"Yes, and of course you can head right over there just as soon as you walk Buttercup. She hasn't been out since early this morning. I can't do it—I'm not allowed to leave the room without my sash on."

I blink. "What?"

"Contestants can't leave their hotel rooms unless they're pageant-ready. Outside of this room, I have to wear my sash at all times."

I don't even know what to say, but suddenly the army of beauty queens from the elevator makes more sense. "That's crazypants. It's like you're some kind of pageant hostage. Put your sash on, and take her out yourself."

Ginny sighs. "Dramatic much? This isn't some tiny regional pageant. *Miss American Treasure* is the big time. She's a role model. You know that."

I do. I probably know more about that than any of those chattering elevator girls.

"I can't go out there like this," she says.

"Fine." I take the leash from her hands. She's clearly in no condition to leave the room, although I would pay money to see an Instagram post of Ginny wearing the sash and her sheet mask at the same time.

"Thank you." Her slender shoulders sag with relief. "I owe you one. We'll have a great dinner tonight, I promise. It'll be just like old times."

Old times?

I don't believe her for a minute. When we were kids, our favorite dinners included sloppy joes and macaroni and cheese. I can't remember the last time I saw a carb cross Ginny's lips.

"Come on, Buttercup," I mutter.

The portly little dog growls the entire time I'm attaching her leash to her sparkly pink collar. This should be lovely.

"We'll be right back." I cast a glance over my shoulder as

I lead Buttercup out the door, and Ginny catches my gaze in the mirror.

She gives me a little wave. I wave back, and for a moment, I go still. Rooted to the spot. Ginny's sheet mask is gone, and her face is bare. Clean. It's been a while since I've seen her makeup-free. Without the airbrushed foundation, the contouring and highlighting, the carefully lined lips and the double layers of false eyelashes, she looks a lot like me.

She looks exactly like me, actually. Same nose. Same eyes. Same heart-shaped face.

Same DNA.

Because even though my sister has always been the pretty one, the beauty queen—the Jane Bennet to my Elizabeth, the Meg March to my Jo—she's also my twin.

2

Ginny and I weren't always such polar opposites. There was a time when we were inseparable. We were the sort of identical twins who dressed alike, wore our hair the same way, and completed each other's sentences. We were twins in the vein of Mary-Kate and Ashley, minus the millions of dollars and a hit television show.

Somewhere in the attic of Dad and Susan's two-story colonial in Dallas, Texas, there are volumes of photo albums documenting this period of my life.

Our lives, I should say.

There was no me back then, just as there was no Ginny. There was just *us*. Me and her. The twins.

On the rare occasion I actually flip through one of those albums, I can never identify myself in any of the pictures. Ginny and I are interchangeable in our matching rompers, matching socks, and matching patent leather shoes. Our haircuts are the same, as are our smiles.

As are our memories.

Was it Ginny who fell off a pony in the kiddie area at the rodeo, or was it me? Which one of us lost a tooth first? Who colored the picture of the house and the smiling family of stick figures that still hangs in a frame above the staircase in our childhood home?

I used to try to sort those early years out, to untangle the web. Then I realized it was hopeless. Being a twin means knowing you're always part of a bigger whole. We were one once, and now we've been split in two.

The day after our fifth birthday, our mom was diagnosed with ovarian cancer. That's when it all stopped—the matching outfits, the photos, the carefully curated albums. Seven months later, she was gone.

I think that's when the split became permanent. Our father had enough on his plate raising twin girls on his own while trying to get tenure at the same time. Making sure we were fed and dressed in clean clothes every morning was a victory in itself. Matching outfits and hair ribbons were out of the question. For the first time, people could tell Ginny and me apart. Somewhere deep down, so could we.

Despite all our similarities, my sister and I handled the loss of our mother in completely different ways. I attached myself to our father—our sole remaining parent—morphing into the quintessential daddy's girl. Other than Ginny, he was all I had left. My love of books is firmly rooted in my childhood and my devotion to my dad, a university English professor.

Ginny loves him too, obviously. She always has. But growing up, she *ached* for our mom. That's what all this pageant business is really about. Our beauty queen mother left a big, beauty queen–shaped hole inside Ginny, and she's been trying to fill it for the past twenty-four years.

I remind myself of this fact when I take up my duties as official pageant dog walker. Buttercup despises me. That much is obvious when she collapses to the ground and tries to writhe out of her collar in order to get away from me the minute the door to our room clicks shut behind us. It's a full-on spectacle, made all the more humiliating by the fact that it's taking place in front of a hallway full of glamazons.

"Stop it," I hiss.

Buttercup flips onto her back and paws at the air. For a second, I wonder if she's having a seizure. But there's a mischievous glint in her googly eyes that assures me she's fine. She's just in the throes of a canine temper tantrum, not a medical emergency.

"Oh my, is your sweet little dog all right?"

I look up. Miss Nevada is teetering toward me on a pair of those mile-high platform stilettos.

More beauty queen interaction is *so* not what I need right now. I let out a strangled laugh. "She's fine. She's just a little shy."

God, I sound like Ginny.

Miss Nevada isn't buying it. "Are you sure? I could take a look at her if you like. I'm a veterinarian."

Seriously? She looks like a petite, Asian-American Barbie doll. No way can I picture her elbow-deep in a pregnant cow. Maybe she's not that kind of vet, though. Still, I'm a little thrown.

"Really?" I say, unable to hide my surprise.

She nods. "First in my class at Cornell."

"That's really impressive." My smile falters. I'm beginning to worry about Ginny's shot at the crown. She's an Instagram model. Meanwhile, Miss Nevada is the Lucy Liu of veterinary medicine.

Not that any of this matters. It's nothing but a plastic tiara covered in cheap rhinestones. Ginny needs to move on and do something real with her life. Something like vet school, or at the very least a dog-training class. Then maybe Buttercup would learn some basic social skills.

"Thanks." Miss Nevada looks me up and down. I can tell she's wondering what I'm doing here, as I'm obviously not a pageant contestant. My face grows hot for some reason, but thankfully she bends to inspect Buttercup, and I breathe a sigh of relief. I'd much rather the dog be the center of attention than me.

Miss Nevada gives Buttercup a once-over as she continues to squirm and grunt. I'm somewhat reassured by this development. Buttercup's disdain apparently has nothing to do with me personally. She doesn't like anyone but Ginny.

"You're right. She seems fine." Miss Nevada stands again. She can't be any more than five feet three, but thanks to her heels, I have to lift my gaze to look her in the eye. "As you said, she's just . . . shy."

It's obvious *shy* is code for something *far* less flattering.

I have a sudden pang of sympathy for the ridiculous dog. We're both outsiders here.

Maybe Buttercup senses this too, because when I squat to scoop her wiggling bulk into my arms, she goes still. For once, she's cooperative. "She's a rescue."

Miss Nevada nods. "Well, my name is Lisa Ng and I'm right down the hall if you need anything."

"Thank you. We're fine, though. Really." I turn and head for the elevator, trying not to dwell on what a pathetic pair Buttercup and I must make.

When the elevator doors slide open, there's no escape. I'm confronted by our reflection in the mirrored walls, and the sight is pathetic indeed. My hair has somehow gone even limper, plastered to my head and neck in damp copper strands. The Hogwarts T-shirt, which seemed so quirky and intelligent a few hours ago, seems juvenile in comparison to the fancy day dresses and sleek suits all the pageant contestants are wearing. The pitiful lump of dog I'm holding doesn't help the situation.

At least we're alone.

Not for long, though. The elevator stops on every floor, picking up beauty queens all the way down. By the time we reach the lobby, I'm pressed against the back wall, choking on hair-spray fumes and a half-dozen different varieties of perfume. It's pretty awful, but just as the descending numbers on the display above the elevator doors wind down to *1*, an aroma much worse fills the confined space. The stench is horrendous, so thick that I can taste it at the back of my throat. Its pungency obliterates any and all lingering traces of flowery perfume and hair products.

And to my great horror, it seems to be coming from Buttercup.

Every head in the elevator swivels in our direction. Perfectly pert noses scrunch in unison. There's apparently no doubt that the source of the stench is either me or the dog in my arms. Miss Idaho presses a hand to her flat stomach, as if she might vomit. I wish I could say it was an overreaction, but honestly, it isn't.

What on earth has Ginny been feeding this creature?

"Sorry," I mumble, longing to feel invisible again. Like usual.

My face burns with embarrassment as the elevator doors slide open and everyone bolts. I'm sure of two things . . .

First, I'm going to murder my sister. Strangling her with her beauty queen sash seems like a really great idea.

And second, for the rest of the week, Buttercup and I will be taking the stairs.

Five hours later, after I've left Ginny and Buttercup behind, I return to the Huntington Spa Resort, as happy as a person can possibly be.

I've spent my afternoon riding the Hogwarts Express, eating an enormous amount of chocolate frogs, and, thanks to the magic of technology and J. K. Rowling's imagination, zipping around on a broomstick through the middle of a Quidditch match. There's an actual magic wand in the back pocket of my jeans, which I used to cast spells all over the park. If butter beer contained alcohol, I'd be sloppily drunk.

Best of all, I'll get to do it all again tomorrow.

My mind is spinning with ideas for the upcoming school year's book festival at the library. It's one of my biggest responsibilities, but also one of my favorite parts of my job.

Last year, the festival's mascot was Skippyjon Jones, the star of the popular children's book series about a Siamese cat who thinks he's a Chihuahua. This year will be all about Harry Potter.

I broke down and purchased a sorting hat from one of the gift shops, simply because I know the kids will love it. Plus I invested in a whole pile of Harry Potter–themed arts-and-crafts books. I spread everything on top of my hotel bed and grin at Ginny, waiting for her to tell me I'm the best school librarian in the state of Texas.

"What's with that huge hat? It's crooked." She crosses her arms.

I don't even dignify this with a response. Honestly, I know she doesn't read much, but hasn't she seen at least one of the Harry Potter films? Or has she been living under a bedazzled rock for the past two decades?

"Do you think it's possible to rent an owl?" I ask.

Her gaze narrows. Or it would, if not for the Botox. "You want to adopt a live owl?"

"No. That would be crazy. I just want to borrow one for the day. For the book festival. Not a regular owl, though. I need a great big white one." I spread my arms out wide to indicate Hedwig's approximate wingspan.

"Right. Because that's not crazy at all." Ginny smirks.

From her perch atop Ginny's pillow, Buttercup rolls her googly eyes at me. I'm clearly outnumbered.

But I'm also in a fantastic mood. A *vacation* mood, so I refrain from pointing out the general insanity of Ginny's pageant obsession. I don't want to argue. Besides, I'm pretty sure she knows how I feel about her quest to become Miss American Treasure.

The title alone is absurd. It sounds more like a Nicolas Cage movie than a beauty pageant. But hey, it could be

worse. Our mother could have been crowned Miss Armadillo Festival Sweetheart. Which, in case you're wondering,
is an actual small-town Texas pageant. I know this because
Ginny contemplated entering it one year as practice for the
big leagues. I managed to talk her out of it when I pointed
out that instead of a tiara, the winner was crowned with a
stuffed armadillo that had been fashioned into a hat. As
much as Ginny loves the pageant life, she draws the line
when the crown involves wearing roadkill on her head.

"Are you ready for dinner? I'm starving." I'd eaten my
body weight in theme park food, but I'd also walked a few
million miles. And unlike every other person in the building, I won't be strutting across a stage in a bikini in the
coming days.

Ginny plops on her bed, crisscross applesauce. She's at
least five shades tanner than she was earlier today, and she's
dressed in a glittering red gingham top, white skinny jeans,
and her Miss Texas American Treasure sash.

She had a pageant luncheon today, where I presume
they served kale or something. She's probably hungry, too.
"Sure. I was thinking maybe we could get some room service, order a rom-com on one of the movie channels, and
have a little picnic. What do you think?"

"That sounds like heaven."

And it is.

We spend the next few hours mooning over Ryan Gosling, laughing and picking food off each other's plates. Ginny meant what she said earlier—it really is like old times.

My twin and I haven't seen much of each other in recent years. After high school graduation, I went away to college at the University of Texas in Austin while Ginny stayed back home in Dallas. It was the first time we'd lived apart, and the distance had seemed even greater as she'd devoted herself full-time to her pageant career and building her social media following while I embraced Austin's laid-back vibe and the campus's progressive atmosphere. As Ginny was modeling swimsuits, I was writing my thesis on feminism in classic literature.

Being away from home changed the way I looked at pageants. I'd never been as crazy about them as Ginny, but they'd always been a part of our family life. Though once I was on my own, I no longer saw them as a sweet family tradition. The more I read and the more I saw Ginny's bikini and tiara pictures pop up in my social media feeds, the more archaic the whole thing felt. I couldn't imagine Virginia Woolf, for instance, competing in a beauty pageant.

When I was home for Christmas junior year, I tried to convince Ginny she needed to do something different with her life, something more meaningful. That conversation didn't go over well at all. We tend to avoid the topic now, but it's always there, hanging between us.

After graduation, I moved back to Dallas and started working at the library. My twin and I once again became a permanent fixture in each other's lives, but things are somewhat strained. As much as I'd like to blame our uneasy relationship on my twin's pageant obsession, I can't. Not entirely, anyway. I just sometimes feel like we're competing against each other, and I'm always the one who ends up losing, while my twin walks away with the crown.

When Ginny learned she'd lucked out and scored one of the few private rooms this week—instead of being assigned a roommate—and invited me to come stay with her, I was a little surprised. I almost said no, but I'm suddenly glad I came to Orlando. It might give us some much needed time away from our usual routines so that we can get back to us, but I shouldn't get my hopes up, since this is probably the last chance we'll get to just hang out together and have fun. Pageant preliminaries start the day after tomorrow.

But for the duration of our little picnic, I forget all about the pageant. It's not until the movie is over and we're getting ready for bed that I'm reminded why I'm actually here.

"Can you take Buttercup for a quick walk?" Ginny yawns and crawls under her covers.

My gaze flits toward her sash, hanging neatly over a hanger in the open closet. Would it kill her to put it on and take her own dog outside?

I sigh. "Sure."

I clip Buttercup's leash to her collar and pick her up before she can repeat her earlier temper tantrum. For obvious reasons, I bypass the elevator and take the adjacent stairwell.

We're about halfway down to the ground floor when I hear another set of footsteps. They seem to be heading in our direction, and I cringe, wondering which state beauty queen I'm about to run into.

I glare at Buttercup. "I swear, if you fart again, you're on your own from now on. Got it?"

She belches in response. Lovely. Why does this dog hate me so much?

We round the corner, and I keep my head down. Maybe if I don't make eye contact, I won't get trapped into a conversation about hair extensions or world peace.

But the first thing I see when I step onto the landing is another dog, and it looks so much like Buttercup that I stop dead in my tracks.

"Wow." I blink. It's another Frenchie mix, or maybe a purebred. The dog is the same blue-gray color as Buttercup and has the same roly-poly eyes and comically oversize ears.

"Twins. What are the odds?"

I drag my gaze from the dog to its owner, who's definitely *not* wearing a beauty queen sash. On the contrary, the person on the other end of the leash is a he, and he's wearing a tie. A very posh-looking tie, silky smooth. I have the irrational desire to reach out and touch it.

"Twins," I echo, because I can't seem to come up with anything else to say. The exact odds of identical twins being born to humans is one out of every two hundred and fifty births, but I'm pretty sure he meant that question rhetorically.

He smiles, and it's a very attractive smile. Very swoon-inducing. This stranger might not be a beauty queen, but he's still pretty. In a chiseled, roguish sort of way, of course. Like Rhett Butler in Armani.

Am I the only average-looking person in this entire hotel?

He nods toward his dog. "This is Hamlet."

A Shakespearean pet name? My librarian heart beats a little faster.

"Let me guess." He glances at Buttercup and lifts a brow. "Fluffy?"

I let out a laugh and shake my head.

"Fang?" His smile widens. "It's Fang, isn't it?"

He's listing dog names from the Harry Potter series, which means he's noticed my Hogwarts shirt. It also means he's more than just casually familiar with the books. Where on earth did he come from? Did I somehow conjure him with my theme park wand?

"It's Buttercup, actually. But I'm rethinking that now. Fang is a much better fit. Thanks for the suggestion."

It's suddenly unbearably warm in the stairwell. I'm consciously aware of the fact that I'm staring at him. I'm studying him so closely that I notice the dimple in his left cheek, hidden beneath the stubble that lines his jaw. I notice the dark rim around his irises—such a contrast to the clear light blue of his eyes—and I even manage to take in the fine weave of his suit jacket.

What am I *doing*?

"Is the elevator broken?" he asks, glancing up the stairs in the direction I've come from.

"No. Just trying to avoid all the pageant hoopla." I tilt my head. "You?"

He shrugs a single muscular shoulder. "Same."

Now I'm certain he can't be real. There isn't a man alive who wouldn't want to be trapped in an elevator with one or more beauty pageant contestants. I know this for a fact.

Buttercup squirms in my arms. She's getting impatient, which is fine. The longer I stand here, the more likely I am to say something ridiculous. "I should probably get Fang downstairs. It's been a while since she's been out."

"Of course." He steps out of my path, and Hamlet obediently follows him.

The two dogs may look alike, but that's clearly where the similarity ends.

"It was nice chatting with you, Hamlet's dad." I give him a flippy little wave.

26

He winks. "Later, Hermione."

And then he's gone.

There are butterflies flitting around my insides. A whole geeky, book-loving swarm of them.

Later, Hermione.

I'm so besotted that I let Buttercup drag me around the perimeter of the hotel three times so she can pee on every palm tree on the premises.

When we get back to the room, Ginny is sitting up in bed, putting lotion-infused gloves and socks on her hands and feet. "What took you so long? I was about to send a search party after you."

"Oh, it's kind of a crazy story . . ." I unclip Buttercup's leash, and the dog bounds straight for my sister.

Only then does the charmed, fluttery feeling fade.

The dog can't get away from me fast enough, which really shouldn't bother me. There's no love lost between us, that's for sure.

But the rebuff reminds me that certain things are better left unsaid between Ginny and me. And even though I'll probably never see the man from the stairwell again, I have a fierce need to keep our brief, meaningless interaction a secret.

Mine and mine alone.

"Never mind," I say. "It was nothing."

3

S ometime in the middle of the night, I'm awakened by a loud gasp.

At first I think I'm hearing things. It's late. The clock reads 3:00 a.m., and after flying to Florida, hitting the theme park, and the slumber party with Ginny, I'd been up for almost twenty straight hours by the time my head hit the pillow earlier. To say I'm disoriented would be an understatement.

So I let my eyes drift closed again, but within seconds, Ginny is shaking me. "Charlotte, wake up."

"No," I manage to mutter.

Has she forgotten that I'm on vacation? During the school year, my alarm goes off every morning at five o'clock. I'm not planning on cracking an eyelid until the Florida sunshine is bright enough to penetrate the thick hotel curtains.

"Charlotte, *please*," she wails. "It's an emergency."

I swear, if she wants me to walk that obnoxious dog in the middle of the night, I'm going to lose it.

"Is the hotel on fire?" I ask, keeping my eyes clamped shut. "It better be."

"*Worse!*" She flips my bedside light on, and I blink against the sudden assault of brightness. "Look at me."

I rub my eyes, and I'm so drowsy that at first I can't tell what she's going on about. *What* is her problem? Did she break a nail? Did one of her meticulously groomed eyebrow hairs grow back overnight?

"Look at my face! What's happening?" She's screaming now, and the panic in her voice, sharp and raw, snaps me into consciousness.

I sit up, reaching for my glasses on the nightstand. Ginny wails again and helps me shove them in place.

"Is it still bad?" she asks.

I blink, certain that I'm either seeing things or that I'm still asleep and this odd conversation is just a dream. No . . . a nightmare.

Because the person sitting on the edge of my bed looks nothing like my beauty queen sister. She's a stranger with a blotchy, swollen face, narrow slits for eyes, and lips at least four times the size of Angelina Jolie's. *Not* in a good way.

I peer more closely, trying in vain to see someone recognizable beneath all the swelling. "Ginny?"

She starts to cry, and I wince. Asking her to verify her identity clearly wasn't the response she was hoping for.

"Of course it's me," she says through her tears. "Who else would it be?"

Out of the corner of my eye, I spot Buttercup shimmying her way underneath the bed. Even Ginny's devoted dog is freaked out by her appearance.

"We need to call nine-one-one. Like, right now." I reach for my iPhone, but Ginny snatches it from my hands before I can push a button.

"No! Are you crazy?" She throws my phone across the room, and it lands somewhere in the pile of sparkle at the foot of her bed.

"Look, I know you're upset. But clearly you're having some kind of allergic reaction. You need a doctor." I reach for the hotel phone on the nightstand, and Ginny swats my hand away.

I swat back at her, and in an instant we are slapping at each other like we did when we were eight, fighting over the haircut I gave her Miss America Barbie.

"Stop!" I leap from the bed, out of striking distance, and cross my arms. "You need help."

"I know that. *Obviously*." She gestures toward her face, which already looks worse than it did just a few moments ago. "But we can't call nine-one-one. They'll send an ambulance, and everyone up and down the hall will see me like this."

I want to slap her again. For real, this time. "Are you

seriously worried about a beauty pageant right now? You could go into anaphylactic shock, Ginny. You could *die*."

For a second, Ginny doesn't say anything. She stands there quietly, and I wait for my words to sink in.

She lets out a deep, shuddering sigh. "You're right, okay. I know I need to get to a doctor. But no one here can see me like this. You can't call nine-one-one. Promise me."

At least she seems to appreciate the seriousness of the situation. "Fine. But get dressed. We're leaving right now."

I'll have to get an Uber or a cab to take us to the closest hospital or something. I vaguely remember passing an urgent-care center earlier in the day on the way to the theme park. It was in a strip mall just down the street. With any luck, they're open twenty-four hours.

I tug on my jeans, sneakers, and my *Talk Darcy to Me* T-shirt—always a hit when I wear it to my boozy Thursday-night book club. Ginny looks at it and shakes her head, clearly not getting the joke. Either that, or the head shake merely represents her general disapproval of my wardrobe. It doesn't matter. I'm just relieved that she's still well enough to judge my fashion sense. Maybe she won't die, after all.

"Okay, let's go." I shove my room key and cell phone in my back pocket and march toward the door.

"Wait." Ginny moves to block my path. She's thrown on a red baby-doll-style dress with tiny white stars scattered over it. She's not wearing her sash, but she still somehow looks like Miss Texas.

From the neck down, at least.

"What if someone out there sees me?" She peers out the peephole on our door.

Seriously? "It's the middle of the night. I'm sure they're all getting their beauty sleep."

She hesitates, lingering by the door.

We don't have time to argue again, and I have the sinking feeling that Ginny might consider death preferable to being seen by her fellow pageant queens in her present condition.

"How about a disguise?" I grab the sorting hat I bought at the theme park and jam it on top of her head.

It's huge, and even with her swollen face, Ginny's head is still beauty queen petite, made for a tiara. There's enough extra room for me to pull down on the brim of the hat so that it covers everything but her chin.

"I can't see a thing." Her voice is muffled by the thick brown felt.

"Good, that means no one can see you either." I open the door and push her swollen, vain self out into the hallway.

We take the stairs because Ginny is convinced the elevator could still be full of pageant contestants—doubtful, considering the hour. But again, I'm too tired to argue. I hold Ginny's hand, guiding her down the five flights as she peeks beneath the brim of the hat.

I can't help but think about the charming man I met earlier in the stairwell, and I wonder what he'd say if he stumbled upon us now. No doubt he'd make some witty quip about the sorting hat. The thought makes me smile, and then my grin fades when another, much uglier thought drifts to the forefront of my mind.

For once, someone would look at us and think that I'm the pretty one.

What kind of monster am I? I bite my lip, hard, as a form of self-punishment. And I give Ginny's hand a squeeze. "We're almost there. Just one more flight of stairs."

At last we reach the ground floor, and the hotel lobby is vacant but brightly lit. Two sleek cars for hire are parked in the valet area, and I offer up a silent prayer of thanks for luxury spa accommodations.

We climb into the back seat of the first town car, and I ask the driver to take us to the closest emergency medical center. He assures me the urgent-care center down the road is indeed open all night, and we're there within minutes.

I don't have to say a word to the woman at the front desk. We walk in, she takes one look at Ginny and immediately ushers us to an exam room. A doctor in scrubs orders a nurse to prepare an IV drip of epinephrine and Benadryl while he shines a light toward the back of Ginny's throat and a third person in scrubs takes her blood pressure. The numbers are frighteningly low.

I wrap my arms around myself and pace the tiny room. *This is really happening.*

What if I hadn't been there? What if I'd been back in Texas and Ginny had been in that room all alone, terrified to leave in case someone from the pageant saw her like this?

My hands ball into fists. This stupid, stupid pageant.

"You're about to feel a shock of cold, followed by a sense of euphoria," the doctor tells Ginny as the nurse ties a tourniquet around her arm in preparation for the IV. He slides his gaze toward me. "Then she'll get very drowsy. I'm assuming you're tourists? You'll need to stay put for a few days so she can sleep this off."

Ginny shakes her head. "Days? No. I—"

"Whatever you say, Doctor," I interrupt, nodding.

The nurse slides the needle in place and attaches the IV tubing. I can tell the moment the medication hits Ginny's bloodstream because her eyes widen and she lets out a loud shudder.

She takes a deep, cleansing breath, and the nurse wraps a blanket around her shoulders.

All my life, I've had to dispel rumors about identical twins feeling each other's pain. Everyone wants to believe that Ginny and I experience the same emotions, suffer the same hurts. It's simply not true. We share the same DNA, but we're two different people. If I cut myself, Ginny doesn't bleed. Just me.

But in this moment, my relief is so profound that I feel my lungs expand along with hers. My sister's breath is my breath, and for some strange reason, I want to collapse into a ball and cry.

"Feeling better?" the doctor asks.

Ginny nods. "I guess I didn't realize how awful I felt until the tightness in my chest went away just now."

"It's a good thing you got here when you did. Your airway wasn't obstructed, but judging by the amount of edema in your face, it was only a matter of time." The doctor flashes me a thumbs-up. "Good work getting her here quickly, although next time you might want to call nine-one-one."

Ginny and I exchange a glance. It doesn't take any special twin magic for her to read my mind. My *I told you so* is coming through loud and clear.

"What do you mean by 'next time'? Is this going to happen to me again?" Ginny wraps the blanket tighter around her trembling frame.

The doctor lowers himself onto a rolling stool and crosses his arms. "You're experiencing an acute allergic reaction to something. Unless you can identify what it was, then yes, this could happen again. The culprit was probably something you ate."

"But we're not allergic to anything." Ginny searches my gaze. "Right?"

The doctor turns toward me. "You're sisters?"

I nod. "Twins, actually. Identical."

"Wow, I didn't realize." He smiles.

We should be accustomed to this reaction. After all, Ginny and I haven't been mistaken for each other in years. It would require Rapunzelesque hair extensions and two hours in a makeup chair for me to look like my sister these days.

This time is different, though. And we both know it.

My heart breaks a little bit, and I can barely look at her, sitting there with tears streaming down her swollen face. I'm used to being the less attractive sister, the invisible one.

Ginny isn't.

"Allergies have a strong genetic component, but they can be tricky. While it's common for twins to be allergic to the same foods, it's not always the case. Did you two share food last night?"

"Yes," we say in unison.

"Then it looks like you drew the short straw, Ginny." He shrugs.

I feel guilty, which I know is absurd. But Ginny is the golden child. The beautiful one. The fact that I'm not the twin who's hooked up to an IV and swollen beyond recognition seems wrong on every level.

I clear my throat. "The swelling is only temporary. She'll be back to normal really soon, right?"

"Absolutely." The doctor nods and pulls a prescription pad from the pocket of his scrubs.

"Thank goodness." Ginny's shoulders sag in relief.

"We've given you a good amount of diphenhydramine in your IV drip. You need to stay here for a couple more hours, so you can get some rest and let it do its thing. But you're going to need to continue taking it in liquid form. I also recommend a course of oral steroids. And you should get allergy tested as soon as possible."

Ginny nods. "Sure. Anything, so long as it works. I need to be onstage by the day after tomorrow. That's possible, isn't it?"

She looks back and forth between me and the doctor. I can't believe she's still going on about the pageant at a time like this. The minute she's stabilized, I'm calling our dad. Maybe he can talk some sense into her.

The doctor's brow furrows. "Onstage?"

"She's a contestant in a beauty pageant." I roll my eyes to indicate my feelings on the subject.

Ginny corrects me instantaneously. "Miss American Treasure. It's a *scholarship competition.*"

I roll my eyes even harder. Who is she kidding?

"I see." The doctor nods. "That's . . . great."

His smile fades, and I know what's coming. "There's no reason you can't be onstage by then, so long as you feel well," he says.

"Perfect." Her puffy lips curve into a smile.

"However . . ." *And here it comes.* "The swelling will likely take a while to go away."

"A while?" Ginny sits up, panicked. The nurse pats her back and tries, unsuccessfully, to get her to lie back down. They might need to put a little something extra in that IV—a tranquilizer, maybe. "How long?"

"It's hard to say. Three days, if you're lucky."

"Three days?" Ginny blinks. At least I think she does— it's kind of hard to tell because her eyes are still nothing but tiny slits. I can't even see her Real Housewives–size eyelash extensions. *"Three days?"*

"If you're lucky." The doctor stands, prepared to bolt.

I don't blame him. I kind of want to slink out the door behind him.

"But I don't have three days." Ginny's voice breaks, and the doctor pauses on his way out.

"I'm sorry. Truly, I am." He looks at me one last time. "I'll give you a call tomorrow to check in and see how she's doing."

"Sure." I nod.

I'll be answering that call from Texas. The minute we get back to the hotel, I'm booking our flights back home. There's no reason to stay here if Ginny can't compete in the pageant, and as much as I need a vacation, I refuse to be trapped in a room with her as she mourns the tragic end of her career as a beauty queen. Frankly, that seems like the worst possible way to spend my summer break.

Until the doctor opens his mouth again and suggests something far more horrendous.

"Since you two are twins, maybe you can take your sister's place in the pageant until she feels better?" He shoots me a wink.

An actual, flirty little *wink*. I don't know whether to be flattered or mortified. What is even happening right now?

"Oh my God, *yes*!" Ginny squeals.

Oh my God, no!

No, no, no. Just . . .

No.

I close my eyes and pray for the floor to open up and swallow me whole. It turns out being the pretty one isn't all it's cracked up to be.

4

"*N*o." I cross my arms and glare at Ginny. "Don't even think about it."

Too late. She's positively wild-eyed with excitement. Aren't the drugs supposed to be making her sleepy? When does the drowsiness kick in?

Because right now she's practically manic with glee. "It's the perfect solution."

"No, it's not. It's a terrible idea." So terrible that I might even sue that quack of a doctor for malpractice for putting it in Ginny's head.

"Why? I mean, it would take some work, obviously. A lot of work." She looks me up and down. "Like a *ton* of effort . . ."

I glare even harder. She's in no position to critique my appearance at the moment.

"But you could totally do it. We'll just need to do something to your hair. And your face. And your lashes. And your—"

41

I hold up a hand. "For the love of God, *stop*."

She gives me the same sympathetic head tilt she uses when she's waxing poetic about sad, unwanted shelter pets. "I'm not trying to be mean, but you know how pageants are."

Yes, I know exactly how pageants are. Which is precisely why I'll never, ever participate in one of them. Has she lost her mind? Just the thought of draping one of those sashes across my body makes me sick to my stomach.

"It's hot in here." I fan myself and start pacing the tiny space again. "I need some water."

Ginny ignores my suffering. Big surprise. "A makeover wouldn't be the end of the world, you know. I don't remember the last time I saw you without a ponytail."

"What's wrong with my hair? You're the one who talked me into these bangs." I gesture at my forehead.

Of course Ginny never mentioned that said bangs would need trimming every three weeks. Who has the time to go to a stylist so often?

"You've been cutting them yourself, haven't you?" If she could move her face right now, she'd be curling her glossed lips in disgust.

How has this medical crisis turned into an all-out war on my image? It's mind-boggling.

"Everyone cuts their own bangs."

"No one does that," she says flatly. "Also, what happened

to those makeup samples I sent you? They were Chanel, for crying out loud."

I can't tell her that I gave them to one of my teacher friends so her daughters could use them for playing dress-up. She'd kill me. "I'm not a makeup person. You know that."

Her retort is brutal. "I also know that you haven't been on a date in over a year."

I rear back as if I've been slapped.

She's going there? Seriously?

Why didn't I call 911 against her wishes and have her paraded through the Huntington, swollen face and all?

"Come on, Charlotte." Ginny's voice goes soft. And, nonsensically, it's the sudden kindness that cuts me to the quick. "Has there been *anyone* since Adam?"

I wrap my arms around myself. *Hold it together.* "I'm not having this conversation."

There hasn't been anyone. Adam is my ex-fiancé, emphasis on *ex*. I'm still not over what happened between us, and I probably never will be. Dating is the absolute last thing on my mind, but I don't want to admit as much to Ginny. She'd never understand. . . .

Probably because I still haven't told her the real reason I called off the wedding.

And I never will.

"I'm not interested in dating right now." My gaze is fixed on the sterile tile floor.

Ginny sighs. "That's what you've been saying for nearly a year and a half."

"Well, it's true." I don't bother explaining that even if I had any interest at all in a relationship, I still wouldn't want a makeover. I'd want to meet someone who was attracted to my inner beauty, not what he sees on the outside.

Does such a man exist?

Not in my experience—hence the dating drought.

"Anyway, what does my love life, or lack thereof, have to do with the Miss American Treasure pageant?" Nothing at all. That's what.

"I'm just saying that if you helped me out it would be good for both of us."

I can see the wheels spinning in her swollen head. She wants to make me over, just like Anne Hathaway in *The Princess Diaries*. And Anne Hathaway in *The Devil Wears Prada*.

Anne Hathaway is spectacularly gorgeous. Why does she keep getting made over? Because the world is a shallow place and all anyone cares about is appearances.

Poor, persecuted Anne Hathaway. I know exactly how she feels right now.

"Stop trying to convince me that you want to do this for my benefit. There's only one reason you want me to take your place." And it's because she wants that rhinestone-covered plastic crown to be placed on her head.

"It's my last chance, Lottie." Her voice goes soft again, and combined with the use of my childhood nickname there's now a vulnerability in her tone that I can't ignore, no matter how desperately I try. "I'm twenty-nine years old."

The age limit for Miss American Treasure is thirty. Next year, Ginny will officially be too old to follow in our mother's footsteps. More specifically, to duplicate her reign.

"There are other pageants." It's a weak argument, but it's all I've got at this point.

"Miss American Treasure is different. I've dreamed of winning this crown since I was a little girl. You know that."

There's a crack in my resistance. I take a deep breath. "We can't, Ginny."

"Why not? Give me one good reason."

I could give her fifty. The problem is that she won't hear any of them. "For starters, it's dishonest. I know you want to win the crown, but you're not a cheater."

I could say that our mother wouldn't want her to win this way, that she and our dad never condoned outrageous ploys like this, but it feels too cruel to utter out loud. It also seems unfair, since I barely remember our mom. But if we do this, it would be lying in a really major way. I know she's desperate, but Ginny is a good person. Switching places is too deceitful even for her to contemplate.

"But it's only for the preliminaries. Winning the finals

would be all up to me, fair and square. You said yourself that I'm a lock for the top twenty. I *always* coast through the prelims. I just can't do it like this." She gestures toward her horribly puffy face. It really does look bad.

I have a hard time believing it will be back to normal in just three days, maybe because I've completely lost faith in her lunatic doctor.

"So go ahead and compete in the prelims. Maybe the whole allergy thing won't matter so much." I can barely get the words out. *Of course* it would matter. They can call it whatever they want, but it's still a beauty pageant.

"I just need help for the first few days. The finals aren't until next week." She makes little prayer hands. "Please."

She shouldn't have mentioned the pageant finals. The final event is going to be televised. My mind is snagging on the possibility of having to stand onstage in front of a bunch of cameras.

What if she's not better by then? Would I have to keep going?

She'd never let me quit. Not if I make it that far and she can't step in.

"Ginny . . ." I shake my head.

She has no idea what she's asking of me.

Maybe if she'd been the sister who'd been compared to her gorgeous beauty queen twin for her entire life, she might. But that's my role. As much as I hate to admit it, even to myself, being Ginny's sister isn't the easiest thing in the world.

Take, for instance, how it wasn't easy in tenth grade when the most popular boy in our class mistakenly invited me to homecoming and then withdrew the offer when he realized I wasn't my twin. Or how it wasn't easy when we turned eight years old and got new dresses for our birthday—Ginny's was pink, glittery, and flouncy while mine was a plain blue, Anne of Green Gables–style pinafore. Or how it especially wasn't easy nearly two years ago when I found out my fiancé was smitten with my twin.

It sounds bad, I know. Ginny has no idea, and I don't want her to find out because it would crush her to know she had anything to do with my failed engagement. But as much as I wish I could forget how it felt to discover that Adam preferred Ginny to me, I can't.

I might never have even known if I hadn't stumbled upon a whispered conversation between him and his best man on the day of our couples' shower.

"Ginny's hot," Adam's friend had said. "Any chance you could set me up with her?"

Adam's response had been a bitter laugh that'd stopped me dead in my tracks. Then, while I stood in the hallway of my parents' house pressed against a wall of Ginny's framed pageant photographs, I heard him admit that, just like that boy in tenth grade, he really preferred my sister.

"No way. I'm hoping to eventually trade up, if you know what I mean." Adam's words had been quiet, but they'd echoed in my head so loudly that I'd wanted to cover my ears. "Swap twins. It's pretty much the only reason I'm going through with the wedding."

I don't remember much after that, other than sliding to the floor and wrapping my arms around my knees as bile rose up the back of my throat. I just know I don't want to feel that way ever again—no one should. So I throw myself into books, the library, and making sure my innocent kids are as prepared for the cruel world as possible because I never want them to feel what I did. And if I focus on them, I don't have to look too closely at me.

Sometimes I think about how much easier life would be if Ginny and I didn't look alike at all—if Ginny could be Ginny and I could just be me.

Would people still compare us?

Would it still hurt so much to always be the sister who fades into the background?

I don't know the answer, but I can't stand the thought of all those eyes on me at the pageant. Being the center of attention is Ginny's thing, not mine. Back when I was engaged, even being the bride-to-be felt uncomfortable. I think about the wedding dress hanging in the back of my closet—the one I can't bring myself to get rid of, even though I know I'll never wear it. Even if I do manage to walk down the aisle someday, I'll never step into that fancy gown again. It's not me.

None of this is me.

"I can't." My gaze drops to the floor in a desperate attempt to avoid the disappointment in her eyes.

But the hurt in her voice is equally hard to endure. "Don't say no. Not yet. We're stuck here for a few more hours. Just think about it."

I don't say anything. There's no way I'm changing my mind. We could be stuck here all night, and my answer would still be the same.

Miraculously, she lets the matter drop.

But it's still hanging there between us as Ginny drifts off to sleep and I'm left in that little room with nothing but the ugly truth to keep me company.

Here's the thing.

Every word I said to Ginny earlier was true. I despise beauty pageants. I absolutely hate them, and it's not as though I haven't given the whole thing a chance.

Before our mother died, when Ginny and I were just four years old, she entered both of us in a beauty pageant for children.

It wasn't the sort of pageant where little girls wear bright red lipstick and fake teeth and huge bouffant wigs like on *Toddlers & Tiaras*. (Those are known as "glitz" pageants, by the way.) Ours was the other variety—a "natural" beauty pageant.

Full disclosure: that's somewhat of a misnomer. Natural pageants aren't totally natural. They're simply less extreme than the glitz ones. Contestants are still likely to wear lipstick and hair spray, just normal amounts of both. Inasmuch as lipstick on a four-year-old can be considered normal.

Anyway, like generations of beauty queens before her, our mom thought it would be a great idea for us to follow in her perfectly poised footsteps. Ask any woman competing for Miss America how she got involved in pageants and I guarantee that at least half of them will say their mothers were pageant girls too.

I suppose some of the moms are the scary, dominating stage mothers everyone hears about. But the majority of them are moms who did the pageant thing with their own mothers and want to continue the family tradition. It's a special kind of sorority. Pageant girls grow into pageant moms who believe that the system instilled them with confidence, grace, and poise. And for the most part that's true.

But there are exceptions to every rule.

News flash! I'm the exception.

My pageant experience was a disaster from start to finish. I tripped on the runway. Not a tiny little misstep either, it was a full-on face-plant. During my talent portion, I forgot the lyrics to "I'm a Little Teapot" and ran offstage, crying.

As my swan song, I peed in my pants during the Sunday-dress portion of the competition.

Need I say more?

It was a long time ago, and while my actual recollection of the mortifying experience is admittedly a little fuzzy, our mother videotaped the entire ordeal. The recording still has a place of honor on a shelf of DVDs in Dad and Susan's living room.

Oh joy.

Needless to say, that was the end of my career as a pageant girl. If our mom had lived longer, I have no doubt that she would have encouraged me to give it another go. I'm sure she would have at least made me stick with it long enough to have a positive experience before calling it quits.

But my mother got sick shortly after my one and only pageant. Even Ginny gave it up for a while—it was like without the pageant mom, she didn't know how to be the pageant daughter. My sister was ten before she found the black-and-white pageant photo of our mom in her Miss American Treasure crown and glittering evening gown with a bouquet of roses in her arms. She carried that picture everywhere she went until our dad finally agreed to let her enter another pageant.

And she's been chasing that crown ever since.

I, on the other hand, found my hope in books. Books were there for me when I was a little girl, growing up without a mom. They saved me, over and over again. I was in third grade, on the afternoon of the Mother's Day tea, one of the first times it happened. I was the only child in the class who didn't have a mother or stepmom. My dad's sister was supposed to come sit beside me during the event, but she got mixed up and showed up at Ginny's classroom instead.

Sitting all alone at that table was one of the loneliest moments of my life. When my teacher realized how upset I'd become, she took me by the hand and led me to the school library. While the other kids celebrated their mothers, I spent the afternoon with Beverly Cleary and Judy Blume. Their words gave me an escape—a place where I belonged. That experience is one of the reasons I decided to become a school librarian. I want to help kids find the same kind of solace and sense of acceptance.

Ginny, however, finds that acceptance in a stranger's applause or a judge's score. My days spent among the stacks mean I'm not required to have a spray tan, painted fingernails, or perfectly coiffed hair. I prefer the scent of ink on paper and old library books to perfume. And while I want to see world peace happen, I'm not convinced that a real-life Barbie can hasten it by uttering those words into a microphone.

So, yes. Everything I said to Ginny is 100 percent accurate. I'm no pageant girl. I also believe that taking her place in the preliminaries would definitely be cheating, no matter how you slice it. We were brought up to be honest, and this flies in the face of everything I try to teach the kids at my school.

But I also love my sister with my whole heart. She's my twin. My other half. As Charlotte Brontë wrote, "You know full well as I do the value of sisters' affections. There is nothing like it in the world."

I'm the first to admit we've drifted apart over the years. It was probably inevitable, considering our diverging paths. But even though I wish Ginny would spend her time on something more meaningful, I'm still there for her when it matters most.

Ginny might drive me nuts sometimes, but I'd gladly give her a kidney if she needed one. I'd do just about anything for her.

So why can't I do *this*?

Because I'm scared, that's why.

It's a humiliating thing to admit—so humiliating that I can't make myself say it out loud.

While I'm fairly certain I could get through the experience without wetting myself this time, there's definitely a part of me that's afraid of letting my sister down. Of disappointing her. Even though we're twins, I was born first. I'm officially two minutes older than Ginny, and this knowledge has always instilled me with a sense of responsibility, especially once our mother passed away. I was the one who cut her sandwiches into the perfect triangles she liked so much for her school lunches. I helped her with her homework. But she missed our mom's influence the most when it came to the "girly" things, like braiding her hair or picking out her prom dress. She cried rivers of tears on our first homecoming in middle school when we were the only girls without "mums," the traditional chrysanthemum corsages Texas is famous for. While all the other girls moved from class to class with streamers, bells, and ribbons fluttering from the enormous flowers pinned to their shirts, we were plain and unadorned. My twin was crushed.

As much as I tried, I couldn't make up for our mother's absence. I still can't, especially if it involves heels and an evening dress. This pageant is the most important thing in the world to Ginny, and while I think it's beyond silly, I'm not altogether sure I could hack it, even for a few measly days of prelims.

After three hours hooked up to the IV, Ginny is released from the urgent-care clinic. She's still drowsy from the massive dose of Benadryl she was given and sleeps for the duration of the short ride back to the Huntington Spa Resort. It's just after six thirty in the morning when I sneak her back up the stairwell and down the hall to our room with the sorting hat jammed on top of her head.

Once we're safely inside, she crawls into bed without asking if I've had a change of heart about the pageant. I should be relieved, but I'm not. Quite the opposite—I feel guilty as hell.

"Buttercup needs to be walked." The poor dog keeps running from the dresser, where her pink leash is draped over a drawer knob, to the door and back. I can take a hint. "Will you be okay by yourself for a few minutes?"

Ginny is a lump in the bed now. She nods, and the covers barely move.

"Okay." I bite my lip. God, she looks so pitiful. "We'll be back in a few."

Buttercup sits somewhat still while I attach her leash, and I let her drag me to the stairwell. The hallway is empty, but I can hear a low murmur of activity behind the doors as the women start their day—it's a mix of blow-dryers, televisions, and beauty queen chatter. The personal interview portion of the pageant prelims is happening all day today, and it starts in less than two hours.

Ginny's interview is slotted for six thirty this evening. At least I think it is. Honestly, I've only halfway been paying attention to the details thus far. But if I'm right, and her interview is twelve hours away, there's technically still time for her swelling to go down. I mean, the doctor didn't *entirely* rule out the possibility, right?

Twelve hours is also undoubtedly sufficient time for me to undergo a pretty thorough makeover, but I push that thought away before it can take root.

Outside, the sun is just coming up, bathing the hotel's fancy cabana and infinity pool in dazzling pink light. In the distance, a row of paddleboats shaped like swans is lined up along the edge of the resort's man-made lake. It's all rather breathtaking, despite the fact that the moisture in the air is so thick that I can barely breathe. Even the palm trees droop a little.

Buttercup starts making a horrible wheezing noise as she picks her way through the grass, and I pause. She's hunched over, frozen, looking like she's having some kind of asthma attack.

Perfect. This is just what I need right now.

"Buttercup, are you all right?" I squat down beside her. She's not all right. The wheezing grows worse, and my heart clogs in my throat.

Nothing bad can happen to this silly dog. Ginny would be crushed, and she's already teetering on the depths of despair.

Just as my concern reaches full-blown panic, I remember Lisa Ng—Miss Nevada, the world's most glamorous veterinarian. Is she in room 520? Or 530? I can't remember. I'm going to have to grab Buttercup, race upstairs, and start knocking on doors.

But just as I reach for the rasping dog, someone else crouches into view.

"She's okay. It's just a reverse sneeze." It's *him*—the man from the stairwell.

I swallow. His calm demeanor does nothing to stop the flutter of my heart, which suddenly seems to be dancing a little rumba in my chest. "A what?"

"A reverse sneeze. It happens sometimes, especially with Frenchies." He cups a hand gently over Buttercup's tiny muzzle and almost instantaneously, the terrible sound stops.

"Wow." I stare at Buttercup for a beat in case it's a fluke, but it's not. She's back to her snooty, buggy-eyed self and continues inspecting every blade of grass in search of the perfect place to relieve herself. "That was . . ."

"Magical?" His mouth curves into a half grin, and his dimple flashes as if it's winking at me. "I think that's the word you're looking for, Hermione."

An unladylike bark of laughter escapes me. *Oh God.* His subtle grin spreads into a full-blown smile. It's every bit as dazzling as the Florida sunrise.

I straighten, fighting the sudden urge to flee. I've been up all night, and I'm still wearing my Darcy T-shirt—which, now that I think about it, is probably a couple of sizes too big. The last time I got a good look at my reflection was a few hours ago in the silvery surface of the paper towel dispenser in the urgent-care exam room. Spoiler alert: It wasn't pretty.

In short, I'm a hot mess. And he's . . .

Well, he's perfect-looking—*again*. He's impeccably put together in a sleek suit and tie, and his hair is slicked back from his chiseled face, still a little bit damp on the ends from his morning shower.

I wonder if he smells good. I'll bet he does. Nice and clean. Manly.

The Old Spice theme song rings in my head like a bell.

What is it about this man that reduces me to such a neurotic train wreck every time I see him?

My face is aflame. "Thank you for the rescue. I didn't know what to do."

"Happy to help. If that's your first exposure to a reverse sneeze, you must be a new dog owner. Or at least new to French bulldogs, I'm guessing." He stands, and I finally notice Hamlet sitting politely by his feet. Together, they look like they walked right off the set of a Hallmark Channel rom-com.

"Sort of." I clear my throat. "Actually, she's not mine. I don't think she likes me much, but we're making it work."

"I see." His eyes narrow, ever so slightly, and I get the feeling he's concentrating on something.

"Everything okay?" I ask.

"Fine. I'm just 'meditating on the very great pleasure which a pair of fine eyes in the face of a pretty woman can bestow.'" The dimple flashes again.

I might faint.

Did he just say I had fine eyes?

Did he just call *me* pretty?

He gestures toward my shirt. I look down at it as if I've never seen it before, even though it's one of my favorites. The words emblazoned across my chest come into focus. *Talk Darcy to Me.*

Of course. He's just parroted Fitzwilliam Darcy from *Pride and Prejudice,* which means he's literally talking Darcy to me. It also means he's complimenting Elizabeth Bennet's eyes, not mine.

The smile wobbles off my face. Of course that's what it means. No one actually talks like that in real life.

Especially not to me.

Still, the fact that he's once again rattling off quotes from my favorite books like they're as permanently ingrained in his head as they are in mine makes me weak in the knees. As does the way he continues focusing on me, even when a flock of pageant contestants glide past us, as graceful as the swan boats bobbing in the distance.

"I'm desperately trying to find a fault in you," I manage to sputter.

It's not an exact quote from the book, but close enough for him to recognize it.

He laughs, and I can tell he's enjoying this little game every bit as much as I am. Off to the side, a few of the pageant girls gather in a cluster. They're looking this way, but his blue eyes are twinkling and he's still smiling.

At me.

My head spins a little, like I've been sipping champagne. Is this what it's like to be noticed? To be *seen*?

If so, I like it more than I should.

"I should go," I blurt.

Ginny is upstairs all alone, and I am running out of things to say to this beautiful stranger. I can't hide behind Jane Austen and J. K. Rowling forever.

"Of course." He nods toward Buttercup. "Best of luck with the dog that's not yours. Don't worry. I have a feeling she'll warm up to you in no time."

"You too." *What?*

He lifts an amused brow.

I square my shoulders and do my best imitation of a person who engages in flirty banter on a somewhat regular basis. "I mean, thanks for the wizardry."

"Anytime."

I turn to head back to the room on shaky legs. The beauty queens linger on the paved walkway, pretending not to watch. But their laughter is too loud, too forced to be real. They've definitely been keeping tabs on our interaction, probably wondering what he sees in me.

To be honest, I'm wondering that myself.

He's just being nice. It doesn't mean anything.

But the heady feeling lingers, and I'm practically floating when I let myself into the hotel room and unclip Buttercup from her leash.

She jumps onto the bed and curls around Ginny with a sigh. At least my sister has gotten something out of this whole pageant mess. I'm 100 percent sure she only adopted that dog as part of her platform, but they look adorable together. Buttercup worships Ginny.

I'm happy Ginny has something real in her life, especially now. Or maybe I just want to believe that she'll be okay without ever winning the crown in order to alleviate my nagging sense of guilt. I pull my cell phone from my pocket so I can call the airline and book our flights back to Texas, but my gaze snags on a framed photo on Ginny's nightstand.

It's the picture of our mother taken the day she was crowned Miss American Treasure. Ginny's brought it all the way here from Texas, and I hadn't even noticed it until now.

I pick it up, studying the smile on my mother's face. It's pure elation. Pure joy. And for the first time in my life, I have the tiniest inkling of what it must have been like to feel like the prettiest girl in the room.

To feel *seen*.

Maybe it wouldn't be so terrible.

I take a deep breath. Could I do it? Could I walk across a stage and hold my head up high while a panel of judges scrutinize everything about me?

I'm not sure I can, but I think I have to try.

For Ginny.

And maybe, just a little bit, for myself.

"I'll do it."

5

"What did you just say?" Ginny's eyes fly open, and she sits straight up in bed as if she'd been lying there just waiting for me to cave.

Oh my God, *is* that what she's been doing? Acting like she's too sickly and pitiful to care about the pageant anymore so I'd feel sorry for her and give in?

What have I done?

Ugh, I played right into her hand. "Don't make me say it again, or I might change my mind."

"Too late." She drags herself out of bed. She's definitely still not herself, but the thought of the pageant at least gets her into a vertical position. "I heard you. We're doing this."

"We?" I lift a brow as she stifles a yawn. "I realize you're running on adrenaline right now at the prospect of transforming me into . . . well . . . *you*, but you're under the influence of massive amounts of Benadryl. Maybe I should try doing this on my own."

"Please." She gives me an exaggerated eye roll and weaves a little from side to side. "Like you could orchestrate your own makeover."

I shrug. "How hard can it be? It's makeup, not rocket science."

Ginny shuffles past me, toward the coffeemaker. "That's what Anne Hathaway thought in *The Devil Wears Prada* until Meryl Streep ate her alive."

Again with Anne Hathaway. Am I the only one who sees what she actually looks like? From now on, I'm watching every movie she ever makes in the theater instead of waiting for Netflix.

That's a promise, Anne!

"Earth to Charlotte. You totally spaced out just now." Ginny shoves a coffee filter into the machine, then turns to face me again. "You can't zone out like that in your interview. You know that, don't you?"

"Of course I do." It's not like I've never sat through a job interview before. I am, after all, employed.

At an actual job, mind you. I don't sit around getting paid for posting photos on social media.

Now that I think about, I'm relieved that the prelims kick off with personal-interview day. Sitting across from a judge one-on-one sounds far easier than flouncing across a stage in platform stilettos and a sparkly dress.

Or, God forbid, a swimsuit.

64

"Oh no." I think I might be sick to my stomach. How could I have forgotten about the bathing suit competition? "I'm going to have to wear a *bikini*, aren't I?"

"Not today." Ginny shrugs.

Only someone like my sister, whose every pore is documented on Instagram, could be this casual about donning a bikini in public.

I try to just breathe and push the swimsuit portion of the pageant to the farthest corner of my mind. After all, Ginny could be better by then.

I take a good long look at her swollen face.

Please, God. Let her be better by then.

"The interview is worth fifty percent of the total score in the preliminaries. So today is crucial." Ginny pours two cups of coffee. The dark liquid fills the Huntington Spa mugs all the way to the rim of each.

She hands me one and I frown into it. "I need cream and sugar."

"Not anymore you don't. From now on, liquid calories are a big no-no."

"I can't lose weight in one day. That's impossible."

She makes her way back to the bed and flops down next to her suitcase. "Care to bet on that?"

What does that even mean?

I'm not sure I want to know, so I take a giant gulp of black coffee. Predictably, it's gross. "Fifty percent seems like a lot."

"Because it *is*. I keep telling you that pageants are about more than just looks." And yet, she's pulling chunks of fake hair out of her baggage and holding them up for inspection.

"Was that suitcase a carry-on, or did you pay good money to check it?" I pull a face.

"They're clip-on hair extensions, an absolute necessity." She gestures at her own head of thick, strawberry-blond waves. "You didn't think all of this was real, did you?"

I'm not that naive, so no. But I'm getting the feeling that the ratio of Ginny's actual God-given hair to her clip-ons is drastically different than I thought it was.

"I've got enough here to get you by." She narrows her gaze to my aforementioned ponytail. Her words are still slurred, but she's got a determined glint in her eyes that's starting to scare me. "*Barely*. But it's going to take a while to clip them all in. And then we've got lashes to do. And makeup. And tanning. How could I forget that?"

Great. I'm going to look like a flaming-hot Cheeto in four, three, two . . .

"The interview is in eleven hours. Oh my God, we're already running out of time."

Seriously?

Eleven hours seems more than sufficient. I was actually hoping to catch a short nap somewhere in there. "But . . ."

Ginny stands, spins me around, and points me in the direction of the bathroom. "Get in the shower. Now."

Before I can take a step, she yanks the ponytail holder from my head. *Ouch!* Then she gives me a weak push and I stumble toward the tub.

This makeover is clearly going to be much more intense than I anticipated.

At least I'll have a few minutes of peace in the shower. After all, I know how to wash myself. I've been doing it all my life.

Or so I thought . . .

My now-caffeinated sister interrupts every five seconds. She peels back the shower curtain, barking instructions and blasting me with a shock of frigid air as she hands me various bottles and tubes of products. There's special shampoo, conditioner, post conditioner, and some kind of hair oil, which I suppose could be considered post-post conditioner.

This seems like overkill, especially since my actual hair is going to be buried beneath a pile of mermaid-length extensions. But I know better than to argue.

Ginny is like a machine. Even while I'm standing beneath the spray of the showerhead, I can hear her whirling through the hotel room, talking to herself and throwing things around. It sounds like someone is getting pummeled in there.

I'm pretty sure it's my dignity.

I'm just about to turn off the faucet and step out of the tub when the shower curtain flies open again.

I jump. "Would you stop? You're going to give me a heart attack."

"Here." She thrusts an elaborate pink handheld device at me.

I turn it over in my hand. "What is this?"

She takes a deep breath, and I can tell she's trying not to strangle me.

"It's a razor—the best electric shaver money can buy. You need to use it." Her gaze flits from my head to my toes. "Everywhere."

I gulp. "Is that really . . ."

"Either do it yourself, or I'm coming in there to take over. Your choice."

God, she's terrifying. Like Norman Bates–level scary at the moment.

"Fine." I slam the shower curtain closed.

Fifteen minutes later, I emerge from the bathroom in one of the hotel's comfy white robes, as smooth and hairless as the day I was born. I half expect Ginny to insist upon a full-body inspection, but miraculously, she takes my word for it.

She sprays something on my hair (post-post-post conditioner?), runs a comb through it, and then applies a generous amount of mousse. I sit and have a moment of reprieve while she wields a blow-dryer—not the one anchored to the hotel wall, but a special, heavy silver contraption the likes of which I've never seen in the budget salon where I get my hair cut.

It's a meticulous process, much more time-consuming than even an upscale blowout bar. She divides my hair into sections, which she winds around a huge, round brush beneath the force of the dryer, over and over again, until it's Christina Hendricks glossy. Like a shiny copper penny.

I stifle a smile. My hair has never looked so amazing, and Ginny's just getting started. After nearly an hour of blow-drying, she drags the desk chair into position right behind me, sits down, and begins clipping the extensions into place.

I'm astounded at the difference they make. Within minutes I'm transformed into Disney's Ariel. The mass of silky, ginger waves extends past my elbows, but somehow still manages to look real. Ginny arranges them in an ombré pattern, so the ends twist into pale, blond curls, with just a hint of strawberry.

The effect is undeniably stunning. I find it hard to breathe all of a sudden.

Then Ginny spins me around, and another three hours pass before I get a glimpse of my reflection.

During this time, Ginny attached tips to my fingernails and applied a variety of serums, mists, and creams to my face and neck. They all come in bottles with lettering I can't read.

"Korean skin care is ahh-mazing," Ginny gushes. "Never use anything else. Promise me."

I nod mutely, unable to speak because I've got something called a collagen lip-plumping patch sealing my mouth closed. It's also Korean and must stay put for the next twenty minutes.

I make a mental note to ask my sister where she's buying all these coveted Asian products. I've never seen anything like them where I buy my Dove face soap, which is the extent of my skin-care regimen. Then again, the odds that I will ever do any of this again are slim to none. I spend my days with books and small children. No one cares how plump my lips are.

Noon comes and goes. Ginny makes a third pot of coffee, and I remind her to take her prescription. Her face looks no different than it did when she was released from the urgent-care center. No better, but no worse either, which I guess is a good thing.

I somehow survive the hour in which I'm forced to stand naked in the bathtub while Ginny applies bronzer to every square inch of my skin. It's humiliating, it smells terrible, and by the time it's all over, I'm shivering like a Chihuahua.

"I'm all sticky. Is it supposed to feel this way?" I slip back into my beloved robe. I swear, when we check out of this hotel I'm taking it with me. It's become my security blanket throughout this ordeal.

"Yes. It means the tan is set. Still, try not to move while it finishes drying." Ginny sweeps me up and down with her gaze. "So far, so good. Now I need to start on your makeup."

Finally.

I'd thought makeup was all I needed. How foolish of me. According to Ginny, makeup is only the icing on the cake—myself being the cake in this scenario.

Cake.

Great. Now I want cake. "I'm starving. Why don't we take a little lunch break first? Maybe order some room service?"

Ginny looks at me as though I've sprouted two heads. I clamp my mouth closed before she seals it shut again with one of her Korean beauty products.

So no lunch, then. Got it.

I close my eyes while Ginny mists my face with foundation from a tiny airbrush machine. It tickles, but I know better than to laugh.

"I'm going to explain the interview process to you while we do this, so listen up." Ginny takes my chin in her hand and moves my face from side to side for inspection.

Then she grabs a large brush and comes at me with bronzer, except she calls it contouring pigment and says it's for minimizing my "problem areas," which are apparently more plentiful than I'd imagined. "The contest has six judges, and each of them will interview you one-on-one for three minutes."

"Three minutes?" I roll my eyes. "That's it?"

Even I can carry on a conversation for three minutes without sticking my foot in my mouth. Piece of cake.

Ugh, now I want cake again.

"It's tougher than you think. The main thing is to keep talking. I mean, don't ramble, but keep the conversation going. A lull in a three-minute interview means you're boring." She gives me a meaningful look. Clearly she thinks I'm more likely to be boring than ramble like a fool. "Miss American Treasure makes all sorts of personal appearances. She has to be able to chat with people from all walks of life."

"Right." I close my eyes again as she goes over my face with a large powder puff. When I open them, I say, "But I'm not actually trying to become Miss American Treasure, remember?"

She lets out a snort. "Of course you're not. That would be insane."

Yes, it would. Very, very insane.

I would never actually want to participate in any of this—interacting with strangers who aren't children isn't my thing. Most adult humans make me anxious.

I adore working in a quiet library, helping kids connect with the books that will eventually change their lives. There's nothing I love more than seeing a child's face light up in anticipation, waiting for me to turn from one page to the next. That's when I know I've found it—the book they've been waiting for. I don't need to look like a beauty queen or an Instagram model to do my job. My students hardly notice what I look like, unless it's Halloween and I'm in my signature Mary Poppins costume.

Still, being on the receiving end of Ginny's incredulous snort doesn't feel great.

I sigh. "Just tell me how it's going to work so I know what to expect."

"It works like a round robin. The contestants are divided into groups of six. At the pre-arranged time, you'll line up with the other five girls in your group just outside the ballroom downstairs where the interviews are taking place." She dips yet another brush into a pot of shimmery silver eye shadow. "One of the title holders from a previous year will be there to help. If you get lost, look for someone in a crown."

As if that narrows things down.

"She'll escort your group into the ballroom when it's your turn. The six judges will be seated at six different tables spaced out around the room. Each of you will walk to one of the tables and stand in front of the chair opposite the judge."

This is all far more complicated than I'd anticipated. "We don't sit down?"

"No," Ginny says sharply. "You stand, so the judge can see how poised and confident you are."

Oh God.

"The title holder in charge of your group will say 'Time.' Then, and *only* then, do you sit down. After three minutes has passed, she'll say 'Time's up,' and you'll move to the next judge's table and do the exact same thing all over again." She shrugs and taps a dab of luminescent white powder on the inside corners of my eyes. My face feels like it has ten pounds of product on it. "Easy peasy."

"Easy peasy," I echo.

But as the minutes pass, my last shred of confidence begins to wane. I put my contact lenses in because Ginny absolutely forbids me to wear my glasses and the next thing I know, she's meticulously applying two rows of strip lashes to each of my upper eyelids. The final touch.

Are we really doing this? Can we pull it off?

Can *I* pull it off?

"Okay." Ginny puts down the eyelash glue. "We're finished."

I swallow. "We are?"

I desperately want to turn around and face the mirror, but I'm afraid. This was a crazy idea. No amount of effort could make me into a pageant girl. I'm a *librarian*. And what we're doing feels more like something from a plot in one of the books I love so much than it does real life.

Even more troubling, I know how those books usually end for characters who lie to get what they want.

"Close your eyes," Ginny says.

I obey and she spins the chair around.

"Open," she whispers.

There's a catch in her voice, and it sends a little shiver down my spine. I open my eyes, look in the mirror, and the world tilts sideways.

It's not me I'm seeing. Those aren't my perfectly arched brows and bee-stung lips. The beautiful girl looking back at me with the dramatic lashes and waves of tumbling hair—miles and miles of it—definitely isn't me. She's my sister. She's Ginny.

It's . . .

Disorienting. And more than a little unsettling.

Ginny places her hands on my shoulders and gives them a squeeze. For the first time since she shook me awake this morning, she smiles. "You look incredible."

I look like you.

I swallow. Hard. And I remind myself there are worse things in the world than looking like my beauty queen twin. Especially in this instance.

After all, that's the whole point of this crazy charade.

6

Half an hour later, I'm lined up with the other five contestants in my group outside the hotel ballroom where the interviews are being held. The temptation to sag against the wall is great. I barely made it downstairs in Ginny's nude patent leather pageant shoes, which could double as torture devices. Or stilts.

I can't help but wonder if some of the time she devoted to my face would have been better spent letting me practice walking in these outlandish stilettos. But every time this thought pops into my head, I catch a glimpse of myself in one of the elaborately framed mirrors hanging on the hotel's silk-covered walls and I reconsider.

The transformation is astounding. The fact that I'm not wearing my glasses might have something to do with how dreamy and beautiful my reflection looks, but not entirely. It's a wonder eleven hours was sufficient.

So I give these heels my all. It's a Herculean effort. I've

been in the shoes less than fifteen minutes total, and I can already feel blisters forming on my pinky toes, my heels, and—is this even possible?—the balls of my feet. Plus, the Spanx contraption that Ginny made me slither into before she zipped me into the retro swing-style dress I've got on makes it almost impossible to breathe.

On the plus side, my waist has never looked so tiny. But I'm mildly concerned I might have cracked a rib.

While I concentrate on taking shallow breaths so I don't burst out of the bodice of my dress, a voice drifts over my shoulder. "Hi there. I don't think we've met. I'm Miss Nevada."

I freeze.

It's Lisa Ng. Veterinarian Barbie!

Also—most inconvenient—the only pageant contestant I've met and conversed with as my regular, unadorned self.

My heart flutters against my rib cage like a butterfly trapped in a net. What if she recognizes me?

I paste a pageant-worthy smile on my face and turn around. "Howdy, I'm Miss Texas, Ginny Gorman."

Inwardly, I'm cringing in horror. Where did the *howdy* come from? Who even am I right now?

"I'm Lisa." Miss Nevada's gaze meets mine. For a second, my inability to breathe has nothing to do with the Spanx. I'm just standing there, waiting for her to call me out on the fact that I'm an imposter or ask me why I've been traipsing all over the hotel with Buttercup for the past twenty-four hours without wearing my sash.

But then her glossy red lips curve into a welcoming smile, and I realize she doesn't recognize me. "Are you ready for your interview? I've been practicing since early this morning."

I swallow. Other than reciting various statistics regarding homeless pets while Ginny helped me get dressed, I haven't practiced at all. But the fact that Miss Nevada doesn't seem to have a clue as to my real identity gives my confidence a much needed boost.

I smile so brightly my cheeks hurt. "I think I'm ready, but is anyone ever truly prepared for these things? You know how it is."

"Do I ever." She laughs. "This is my third time in a national pageant. What about you?"

Her third time? She's stunning. And she's obviously smart, not to mention the whole saving-animals-for-a-living thing. How has she not been crowned Miss Universe or something by now?

I shrug. "Third or fourth. I'm beginning to lose count."

I have no clue if this is accurate information. At any given moment, Ginny's either in a pageant or she's preparing for one. How am I supposed to keep track of what she's got scheduled in her rhinestone-encrusted bullet journal?

But thank God that due to her obsession with following in our mother's glittering footsteps, I know her history with the Miss American Treasure pageant like the back of my hand. All the other pageants are a blur. Surely this isn't going to come up in the interview?

Hopefully not, but maybe I should try to invent a timeline, just in case. Before I have a chance to give this any thought, someone shouts my name.

Correction—my sister's name.

"Ginny! Omigod, I've been trying to reach you all day. Where have you been hiding yourself?" A blonde with the biggest updo I've ever seen throws her arms around me, and I get a mouthful of Aqua Net.

I squint while I hug her back because her chignon is seriously stiff enough to poke an eye out.

"I haven't been hiding." *Liar, liar pants on fire.* "Just getting some beauty rest."

Beauty rest.

I sound like a 1950s housewife. Does my sister actually talk like this? Does anyone? Other than those silly Miss-American-Treasure-do-not-disturb tags, I mean.

"You look perfect, as always." She sweeps me up and down with her gaze, and I hold my breath.

But like Miss Nevada, she seems to be perfectly content believing I belong here. She's obviously one of Ginny's friends, and she *still* doesn't realize I'm a fake.

"Seriously, you look amazing," she says.

"Thank you." I beam. Then it dawns on me that she and Miss Nevada haven't said a word to each other.

"So sorry. Where are my manners? Lisa, have you met . . ." For a second, I panic. My gaze flits to the blonde's sash. These things are basically name tags. *Thank God.* ". . . Miss Arkansas?"

They introduce themselves to each other, and soon we're chatting like a trio of sorority sisters. I can't quite believe they both think I'm Ginny. If this is my first test, I'm passing with flying colors.

Miss Nevada wrings her hands and lowers her voice. "I've heard these judges are pretty tough. My roommate came back from her interview this morning in tears."

Miss Arkansas goes pale.

"She was *crying*?" The bird in my chest flutters its wings again.

Miss Nevada nods. "It was brutal, apparently. One of the judges didn't ask her any questions at all. She just handed her a mirror and told her to spend three minutes describing the person she saw in her reflection."

What kind of hellish mind game is *that*?

I panic for a beat, trying to figure out what I could possibly say about the person I'd see in the mirror.

She's a phony.

She's a wreck.

She doesn't belong here, no matter how beautiful she looks on the outside.

I think I might pass out.

"Six judges at three minutes apiece is only eighteen minutes." Miss Arkansas's perfectly lined eyes turn steely. "Eighteen minutes is nothing. We can do anything for eighteen minutes, right?"

"Of course we can," I say, but it comes out sounding more like a question than an affirmation.

Eighteen minutes is about the same amount of time I've been standing in the sky-high pageant shoes, and I'm pretty sure my feet are bleeding. So yeah, it's quite a bit longer than she thinks it is.

Maybe Lisa realizes just how daunting eighteen minutes can be, though. Because she's still dwelling on the mirror question. "It just seems like such an unfair tactic, don't you think? I mean, they've got our entire life right in front of them. The questionnaire was definitely thorough."

I agree with her because it seems like the appropriate thing to do. "I know, right?"

But my mind snags on something she said, and a whisper of dread snakes its way through me. Ignoring Ginny's strict order to smile at all times, my face falls and I frown. "Wait. What questionnaire are you talking about?"

"Are you kidding? How could you forget the All About Me information sheet?" Miss Nevada eyes me like I'm an elderly lapdog with a memory problem. "We turned them in last month along with all the other entry forms. It was three pages long. I felt like I'd written my autobiography by the time I finished filling it out."

Miss Arkansas nods. "You and I filled them out together, Ginny. Surely you remember."

My face goes hot, and I fear my sash might spontaneously burst into flames, exposing me as the liar that I am. "Oh *that* questionnaire. Of course! What a nightmare."

Great. Ginny didn't say a word about a questionnaire. But if it's titled "All About Me," I've got to be familiar with whatever answers she provided. Ginny's my twin. I know everything about her.

Still, a heads-up would have been nice.

"Attention, ladies." A woman with an enormous, dazzling tiara balanced on her waves of chestnut hair extensions claps her hands, and we all swivel our heads in her direction. The words on her sash are spelled out in red, white, and blue rhinestones, and they read, *Miss American Treasure 2013*. "My name is Jordan Collins, and I'm the title holder assigned to your group."

She's a dead ringer for Beyoncé. There's a smattering of applause from the half dozen of us assembled, and every eye is glued to her glittering crown.

Even mine.

It's exactly like the one in the photograph of my mother

on Ginny's nightstand. My eyes go a little misty, which I blame on sleep deprivation. I can't possibly be getting emotional over a beauty pageant.

Somewhere in the back of mind, I hear Ginny's voice. *It's not a beauty pageant. It's a scholarship competition.*

"Your personal interviews will begin in one minute. I'll open the door, and you're to enter the ballroom as instructed yesterday at the pageant orientation luncheon. Any questions?"

Indeed, I have a million questions.

Mainly, what the hell am I doing here?

"Good luck, y'all. I'm sure you're both going to do great." Miss Arkansas squeezes my hand, along with Miss Nevada's, and then dashes back to her own group, which is lined up directly behind ours.

"Thanks," I say.

Why is my heart beating so hard? This pageant isn't important to me at all. I'm just a placeholder until Ginny gets better.

"Here we go," Lisa whispers behind me when Beyoncé opens the door to the ballroom.

I can barely breathe. I think I might be hyperventilating as we walk single file inside the ballroom. Thankfully, I'm the third in line, which gives me the opportunity to watch how the girls in front of me peel off and go stand in front of the first two judges' tables.

It feels like I'm moving in slow motion, probably because I can barely take a step in my beauty queen shoes. I'm a newborn giraffe in a room full of gazelles.

The judge at the third table is clearly a former pageant queen, so pretty she barely looks real. She meets my gaze but doesn't crack a smile as I come to a stop directly in front of her. My stomach plummets, and I just know she's going to pull out a hand mirror and ask me to wax poetic about the girl I see in its reflection as soon as I take a seat.

"Time," Beyoncé says, and maybe it's just my imagination but she actually sounds a lot like the real Beyoncé.

Focus.

I perch on the edge of my chair, knowing without a doubt that if I sit back all the way I'll never be able to haul myself into a standing position in these shoes again.

"Howdy, I'm Miss Texas." Again with the howdy. Who. Am. I?

Even my voice sounds different—too loud, too animated. But the judge seems to like it, if her sudden smile is any indication.

"Good evening," she says. "Why don't you start by telling me how you got involved in pageantry?"

"Oh." I sit up a little straighter. *I know this!* "It's a family tradition."

I go on to explain that more than three decades ago, my mother won this very pageant. Then I tell the judge how

I'm competing in her memory. I tell her about my mom's illness and what it was like growing up without her.

I'm telling Ginny's story, obviously. Not mine. But as I go on to describe the photograph of our mom on the night she was crowned, my throat grows thick.

Maybe it's the exhaustion, or maybe it's the fact that I look so much like Ginny that the line between our two identities has grown blurry once again, but the story feels as much mine as it does hers this time.

With one important difference—I leave out the part about being an identical twin. I don't mention Ginny at all. It seems like the wise thing to do, in light of the circumstances. But it also leaves me feeling strangely untethered, as if I've willfully erased her existence. Or mine . . .

I'm not entirely sure which.

"Oh my." The judge's eyes brim with tears, and she places a slender hand on her heart. "What a lovely story."

She jots something down in the white three-ring binder in front of her, and I get the distinct feeling that's a good thing.

I'm nailing this.

"Time."

All the contestants stand, and we each rotate to the next table.

Judge number two looks vaguely familiar. When Beyoncé calls time again and I'm allowed to sit, I finally recognize the judge as the host of a syndicated morning talk show. I'm pretty sure she's a former Miss America.

"Good evening, Miss Texas." Her gaze is impassive. She glances down at the binder in front of her—identical to the one the other judge had—and back up at me. "Tell me about your animal-rescue platform."

Aha. I know this, too.

I parrot all the information Ginny made me memorize about the homeless pet population and then launch into a vivid description of Buttercup, "my very own rescue dog." It might sound like I'm pouring it on a little thick when I mention how her eyes seem to point in two different directions, but it's true.

Miraculously, the judge cracks a smile.

I barely have time to answer another question before our three minutes is up. Again, I move to the next table feeling triumphant. This is going so much better than I expected. I can't wait to get back to the room and give Ginny the good news.

Judge number three—a fashion designer who specializes in pageant gowns—catches me a little off guard when she asks me to tell her something surprising about myself. I take a gamble and tell her that I peed in my pants at my very first pageant. She laughs so loud that heads turn in our direction.

Three down, three to go, I chant to myself when it's time

to switch tables again. The next judge repeats the question about how I got involved in pageantry, and again I share the story about my mother. By the time I finish, she's reaching for a Kleenex. While she dabs her eyes, I can't help but glance back at Miss Nevada.

She's slipping her arms over her head backward, like a contortionist or a Cirque du Soleil performer, I'm pretty sure in response to the "tell me something surprising about yourself" question. The fashion designer judge is staring at her in horror. My heart sinks a little bit on Lisa's behalf.

Keep your eye on the prize. You're almost finished.

I refocus on the person sitting across from me and gush about how walking shelter dogs once a week has changed my life, leaving out the part about Buttercup throwing herself on the ground and faking a seizure.

"Time."

The next interview goes just as well. The judge is a man this time—a former contestant on *The Bachelorette* and *Dancing with the Stars*. If memory serves, his cha-cha was abysmal. Plus, to be honest, I'm a little creeped out by the fact that he's a man. A guy judging women in swimsuits seems a little pervy.

Right?

But he's an animal lover, and he melts into a puddle of goo when I tell him about Buttercup and my volunteer work walking dogs at the shelter.

Only one more judge to go.

I don't walk to the next table. I *float*. My feet barely touch the ground. How could I have been so nervous? I'm breezing through these interviews. There hasn't been a single lull in any of the five conversations I've had thus far. Each one felt like it ended right after it had begun.

In the seconds before Beyoncé calls time again, I'm so busy mentally high-fiving myself that everything seems to blur into a misty, glittering dream. I can't believe I'm actually pulling this off, and I have to admit that it's not quite as mortifying as I thought it would be.

But then the judge at the table in front of me looks up, and once again, the room comes into sharp focus.

My knees wobble. I'm no longer floating. I'm barely standing upright. Because the man looking up at me—the one who has a little gold badge pinned to his lapel with the word *Judge* engraved on it—isn't a stranger.

It's *him*.

The man from the stairwell. Hamlet's dad.

This isn't a dream at all. It's a nightmare.

"Time."

I can't seem to sit down. I can't seem to move at all. I'm paralyzed.

Breathe. Just breathe. He has no idea who you are.

Of course he doesn't. The last time he saw me, I was wearing my glasses and one of my oversize nerdy, book-

89

lover T-shirts. There wasn't a speck of makeup on my face and, as Ginny so lovingly pointed out, my hair was scraped back in its usual ponytail.

I'm unrecognizable. Completely incognito.

Still, I'm shaken, and when I finally sink into the chair, it's with an audible thud.

The corner of his mouth tugs into a half grin, and I catch a flash of the familiar dimple in his left cheek. My heart flutters. My stupid, stupid heart.

Say something.

"Howdy. I'm . . . I'm . . ." I stumble over my tongue. Heat crawls up the back of my neck.

I've never felt more like a fraud.

Say it. Just say it. I'm Miss Texas.

"I'm . . ." I smile. At last I've found my voice, but before I can form the words, he finishes for me.

"Hermione."

7

I could deny it. I *should* deny it.

I know I should, especially when he studies me more closely, clears his throat, and says it again as a question rather than a statement of fact.

"Hermione?"

A glimmer of doubt is buried somewhere in the startling blue depths of his eyes, and I get the definite feeling that if I pretend I don't understand what he's talking about, he'll drop it. He'll realize I'm not me, and we can move on and proceed with the interview.

Except I *am* me.

My hair isn't mine, and neither are my lashes, my nails, my clothes, or these godforsaken shoes, but beneath all the sparkle, I'm still me.

Charlotte.

This awareness is more disappointing than it should be. Crushing, actually.

I've had no trouble at all impersonating my twin for the past half hour. Pretending has been ridiculously easy. But suddenly, passing myself off as Ginny seems impossible.

It's as if I've told so many lies that I can't force another one out of my mouth.

I swallow. Hard. *This will be the lie that breaks me.* "Um . . ."

My hesitation is the only answer he needs. His smile is full wattage this time. "I knew it was you."

My insides do a bouncy little dance. How did he know? How could he have possibly seen the real me? I'm desperate for the answer, but I can't ask. Obviously.

"My real name is Ginny Gorman." I dig my fingernails into my palms. I'd almost said *Charlotte*. "Miss Texas."

"Of course." He nods, and his smile dies a little on his lips.

I wait for him to officially introduce himself, but he doesn't. He seems almost as thrown as I am by my sudden appearance at his judge's table.

An uncomfortable, excruciating silence stretches between us. I glance at his name tag.

Gray Beckham.

My stomach does a little tumble.

The book-quoting charmer has an actual name, and it's not Fitzwilliam Darcy. My literary heart should probably be disappointed, but it's not. Gray Beckham is an undeniably sexy name. Very manly. Very 007.

God, what is wrong with me?

The heat in my face intensifies.

Say something.

This is officially the longest three minutes of my life. A million things I should be saying right now are spinning in my head, but I can't seem to articulate any of them. I just want to ask him questions.

Tell me about yourself, Mr. Beckham.

Ginny is going to murder me.

"So." He shifts his gaze to the binder open in front of him. "It says here that you're . . ."

I take a deep breath. Thank God for the questionnaire. At least it will give us some talking points.

" . . . an Instagram 'spokesperson.'" His brow furrows ever so slightly.

I can hear his air quotes dangling around the word *spokesperson*. We both know that's code for *model*. He probably thinks there are a million bikini pics of me all over the internet.

There wouldn't be anything wrong with that, obviously. What a woman does with her body is her own choice. Go, feminism!

It's just very much not me, and I can tell he's struggling to reconcile this image with the one of me speaking to him in book quotes, wearing a Hogwarts T-shirt, and blushing furiously at the nickname Hermione.

Not that I can blame him. I'm trying to figure out how to wrap my own mind around it long enough to make him believe it makes sense.

"Yes." I nod. "But it's only temporary."

What am I saying?

"I'd like to be a librarian someday." I'm treading on thin ice, skating between an identity that's neither mine nor Ginny's. What's worse is I don't even know why I'm straying from the script.

Yes, you do, a tiny voice whispers from somewhere deep inside.

I don't want to feel invisible again. Not now. Not with him. I want him to see me. The real me.

I like him. So much so that I decide to overlook the fact that he's a pageant judge.

God knows why. I barely know the man. I just know that the few encounters we've had have left me breathless. And I haven't met a man who I've found interesting in a long, long time. I slammed the door on romance the day I shoved my wedding gown to the back of my closet. But somehow our quirky conversations have cracked that door open. Just a smidge. Barely enough to let the light in . . .

But that's something, isn't it?

"A librarian. I can see that." He lets out a laugh, and for a moment I'm back in that stairwell with my heart in my throat as he winks at me. *Later, Hermione.* "So what's your favorite book?"

"Wow, that question is almost impossible. I love the Harry Potter series. And Austen." I flash a smile. "As you know."

Oh my God, I'm *flirting.* This has to be against the rules.

Right, like you haven't already broken every pageant rule in existence by now?

My palms are sweating. And I know I need to reel it in, to get things back on track, but I can't.

"But if I had to choose just one, I'd probably say *Jane Eyre.* I read it when I was eleven—my first classic—and I've been in love with it ever since. It's my comfort read. I always pick it up when I'm feeling down." I swallow. "Or lonely."

I've said too much. All notions of sticking to the script are out the window. I don't know what's happening. It's like I've been given some sort of truth serum.

But he seems intrigued. He leans in close, and I go a little breathless. Who is he, and what's he doing here? Chiseled good looks aside, he seems almost as out of place as I do.

I steal a glance at his binder, just in case his bio is in it somewhere. It's not.

When I look back up, I realize he's followed my gaze and is now inspecting the papers in front of him—the dreaded questionnaire, which all my previous judges ignored, for the most part.

He meets my gaze again, but this time, there's not a trace of warmth in his expression. "It says here your favorite book is *Fifty Shades of Grey*."

Oh. My. God.

Seriously, Ginny?

"Oh, well, that . . ." How can I possibly make sense of that answer after all I've just said?

He interrupts before I can give it a try. "It also says that your platform is animal rescue and that part of your volunteerism in that regard has been adopting a French bulldog mix."

He's changed the subject. *Thank God.* Nevertheless, something about the tense set of his jaw sends a trickle of dread coursing through me. What else has Ginny written on those pages?

The problem isn't with Ginny's answers, though.

"Would this be the same French bulldog mix that I've seen you walking around the premises?" He lifts an accusatory brow. "The one you said doesn't actually belong to you?"

Great. Now he thinks I'm a liar.

My face goes hot. I'm no longer a beauty queen with aspirations of being a librarian. I'm a lying liar who lies and also has horrible taste in literature. "Not really."

His gaze narrows. "So you've got another Frenchie mix tucked away somewhere?"

"No, just the one. The situation is a bit complicated."

My smile freezes in place. I've heard better excuses from elementary school kids who lost their library books.

"Is it?" He angles his head, and an angry knot forms in his perfect, square jaw.

He's giving me the full Mr. Darcy treatment now. Not the evolved Darcy who meditates on fine eyes and takes a sexy plunge in the pond at Pemberley, but the haughty, judgmental Darcy from the first half of *Pride and Prejudice*. Any minute now I expect him to declare that I'm tolerable, but not pretty enough to tempt him.

Scratch that. I probably don't even rank as tolerable since nothing on the questionnaire rings true.

"The dog is mine. I was joking earlier. It's a little game Buttercup and I play. We pretend not to know each other," I say in an attempt to salvage any small shred of this interaction.

But it's a ridiculous assertion, and now I sound crazy in addition to deceitful. I cast a desperate glance at the timekeeper. How has she not called time yet? This is officially the longest three minutes of my life.

"This is really too bad." He closes the binder. It feels fatal somehow, as if Ginny's lifelong dream has just died. Because I killed it.

Tears pool in my eyes. Why was I ever foolish enough to believe I could do this? The pageant . . . the flirting . . . all of it has been such a foolish mistake.

"I thought you were something special." His gaze bores into mine, and I know without a doubt that we're no longer talking about the crown. Nor Ginny.

We're talking about me.

My lips part, and I'm not entirely sure what I'm going to say. I just know I can't leave things like this. "I . . ."

But I'm too late.

"Time."

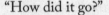

"How did it go?"

Miss Nevada is hot on my heels the minute our group exits the ballroom. She obviously doesn't realize I'm dying inside, because she's giving me a blow-by-blow of her answers and nodding excitedly.

"I think I did really well," she gushes. "How about you? I noticed a few of your judges reaching for the Kleenex. Crying is a sure sign that you nailed it."

Right. Except at the moment, I'm the one on the verge of tears. My eyes brim with humiliation, but at the same time, a swell of anger is rising up inside me.

"I need to go." I turn on a wobbly heel and walk away before Miss Nevada can ask me what's wrong.

The hotel is packed wall to wall with contestants, and I can't stomach the sight of any of them right now. I push past them as quickly as I can, but it's not fast enough, so I commit the cardinal sin of removing my shoes once I get to the lobby. Miss New York, Miss New Jersey, and Miss Rhode Island are gathered in a glamorous little trio just inside the elevator bank, and all three of them freeze in alarm at the sight of my nude patent leather stilettos dangling from my hand. I might as well be walking through the hotel stark naked.

Taking my usual route, I head for the stairwell. Alone at last inside the sterile concrete chamber, I break down. I'm shaking with rage. I realize what just happened is 100 percent my fault. I lied, plain and simple.

What kind of person pretends to adopt a dog? Not one who wants to be a role model, that's for sure.

But did he have to be so haughty in his assessment of me? It's a *beauty pageant*. Or a scholarship competition. *Whatever*. It's not like this is actually important.

Except it is. To my sister, at least.

And now I have to go back to our room and tell her that judge number six thinks she's faking the whole animal-rescue thing. Or that *I'm* faking it . . . whatever. I'm not sure which one of us is actually competing anymore. I just know that it's been less than an hour since I started walking in my twin's beauty queen shoes and I've already made a mess of things.

It's over.

I'm not doing this anymore. I can't. There's no way I can face that man again. I'm done.

Ginny will be disappointed, but she'll get over it. It's not like she can be a beauty queen forever. She's going to have to move on eventually.

Besides, I tried. I really did.

By the time I trudge up the final flights of steps, I've made up my mind. Now I just have to break the news to my sister, which I'm going to do immediately. Quickly. Like ripping off a Band-Aid. Or in this case, double-sided wardrobe tape.

"You're back!" Ginny is wrapped in one of the hotel's plush robes and tucked into her bed when I walk into the room. Buttercup is curled against her hip, and the television is blaring. Kylie Jenner's lips take up half the screen.

Before the door has a chance to click shut behind me, Ginny sits up, aims the remote at the flat screen, and the television goes blank. "How did it go? Tell me *everything*."

I take a deep breath and climb onto the bed, beside her. Soon we're propped up on pillows with our heads resting against the headboard, side by side. Just like when we were kids.

"Well? Don't keep me in suspense," she prompts, swiveling her face toward mine.

She's putting on a good show, pretending to be excited

about the interview. But at such close range, I can see her red-rimmed eyes. Her puffy face is tear-streaked, and there's a pile of wadded up Kleenex on her nightstand.

She's been crying.

"It was . . ." I swallow. Hard. "It was okay, I guess."

Good job, Charlotte. Way to rip off the Band-Aid.

Ginny deflates a little bit, and I try not to notice how tiny she looks in that big, fluffy robe. So sad and vulnerable.

I'm not going to lie. Seeing her this way gets to me. I can't remember the last time I saw Ginny cry.

"Just okay?" She blinks, and her eyes go shiny.

I look away, but my gaze flits automatically to the television screen, where I can see our reflection. Two sisters, shoulder to shoulder. Only it's as if we've switched bodies. I'm undeniably pretty and polished, and Ginny is a mess. She's in even worse shape than when I left her here a couple of hours ago.

I drop my gaze to my perfectly manicured hands, folded neatly in my lap. "Actually, the first five interviews were pretty great. I brought a couple of the judges to tears."

"What?" Ginny squeals. "That's amazing!"

I have to remind myself that none of this matters. I'm quitting. But my heart gives a joyful little tug. It *was* pretty amazing. Until the last three minutes, anyway.

"But I totally blew it on the last one," I say.

"That's okay." Ginny shrugs. "A bad score from one

judge won't keep you out of the finals. If five out of six liked you, you're still in this."

I correct her at once. "You mean *you're* still in it."

"I think I meant *we*." She gives me a conspiratorial grin. "*We're* still in this."

She has a point. He's only one judge out of six. And I know I crushed it on the first five interviews.

Do I really need to throw it all away? Do I really *want* to?

I let out a weary sigh. "What if he talks to the other judges and tells them I'm a train wreck?"

She shakes her head. "He can't. The judges aren't allowed to share their scores with each other. They can't discuss the contestants' performance at all until the pageant is over and the winner has been crowned."

Okay, this is important information. Total game changer.

"What went wrong, anyway?" Ginny asks. "With judge number six?"

"Everything." There's only so much I can say, since I never told her that I've been flirting with a total stranger while I've been walking her dog. "You didn't tell me about the questionnaire. He asked me about my favorite book."

I slide my gaze over to Ginny and smirk. "*Fifty Shades*? Seriously?"

She gives me a blank look. "Everyone loves that book. It sold something like a million copies."

Well, 125 million, actually. My librarian soul weeps every time I think about that statistic.

"I know, but why on earth would you choose something so . . . so"—I want to say *embarrassing*, but I also don't want to sound like a Puritan, because I have a feeling that would lead to a discussion of my dating life, or lack thereof. And I can't have that conversation. Not now, not when I've just been so thoroughly rejected by the only man I've been remotely interested in since Adam—"controversial?"

"That's precisely why I chose it. Miss American Treasure should be a strong woman with a strong opinion. I would have defended that book by talking about how empowering it was for a lot of women."

It's an interesting take. It's also one I never would have come up with on the fly. "A heads-up would have been nice."

"Sorry. I didn't think to go over the questionnaire. Anyway, I figured your answers wouldn't be a problem." She shrugs. "You've always been the smart one."

The smart one.

I've never thought of myself that way. All this time, I've been so painfully aware of Ginny's reputation as the pretty one that I haven't for a moment considered how I fit into the equation.

Maybe I haven't been as invisible as I'd thought.

The smart one. It sounds like a compliment, but I know better. If I'm the smart one, that means Ginny is the opposite—the dumb one. I know this as surely as I know what not being the pretty one means.

I reach for my twin's hand and squeeze it tight.

She squeezes mine back, and I know without a doubt that I can't quit the pageant. Switching places might not be such a bad thing. It might even be the best thing that's ever happened to us.

Like it or not, I'm in this for the long haul.

8

When I wake up the next morning, the two most frightening words in the English language are spinning in my head.

Swimsuit competition.

I'm fully aware of how shallow that sounds. Obviously, there are more frightening issues facing the world than the two scraps of emerald-green Lycra my sister calls a bathing suit. But at the moment, none of them loom as large.

"Do I have to wear a bikini?" I whine, casting a longing glance at Ginny's luggage. "Don't you have a one-piece in there somewhere?"

Or better yet, a burka?

"Ew, no." Ginny pulls a face. "This isn't 1930."

There are a dozen ways I could dispute her comment, starting with Farrah Fawcett's famous red one-piece from the seventies, but why bother? There's not a maillot in sight.

Just tiny bits of fabric that look more like lingerie than anything I'd wear to the beach.

"Um, does this top actually have a push-up bra inside it?" I recoil.

I can't believe I let a brief moment of sisterly bonding convince me to keep going in the pageant.

"Just try it on. You'll look amazing. Trust me." Ginny crosses her arms and glares at me.

The good news is that her face looks a tiny bit better today. The swelling has gone down a smidge, and she's not quite as blotchy as she was the night before. It's almost enough to convince me there's an actual light at the end of this rhinestone-encrusted tunnel.

But not soon enough.

I slither into the bikini and emerge from the bathroom, afraid to face the mirror.

"You look great," Ginny says.

I cast a wary glance over my shoulder at my reflection, but then Ginny orders me to stop. "Don't. This isn't the one. You look great, but we can do better." She rummages around in her bag and pulls out another, more minuscule option. "Try this."

"Ginny, I . . ."

"Do it!" she shrieks, and Buttercup shimmies her way under my bed.

"Fine." I snatch the suit from her hands. What's another quarter inch of skin when I already feel practically naked?

On my way back into the bathroom, I catch a glimpse of myself in the vanity mirror, and I have to admit, I look pretty good. Not Victoria's Secret–model good, but decent enough that I won't necessarily embarrass myself.

Unless I fall on my face, which is a definite possibility. Apparently I have to wear the nude patent leather platform stilettos again. Maybe Ginny's wrong. Maybe this is, in fact, 1930.

"I can't believe the swimsuit competition is still a thing." I emerge from the bathroom again, bypass the mirror altogether, and give voice to the rant that's been building in my head all morning. "Isn't it a little antiquated? Not to mention sexist?"

Ginny sighs. "If it makes you feel any better, most major pageants focus on body positivity now. You'll see women of all shapes and sizes out there on the runway. How you look in the swimsuit doesn't matter nearly as much as how much confidence you exude when you strut your stuff."

My stomach turns. I've never strutted a day in my life. "Is that true?"

"Yes. I promise. You could look like a *Sports Illustrated* swimsuit model, but if you dash off the stage as quickly as you can and avoid eye contact with all the judges, your score will be miniscule."

I narrow my gaze at her. "As minuscule as this bikini?"

She bursts out laughing. At least one of us is enjoying

this experience. "Turn around and look at yourself, would you?"

Eyes closed, I take a few deep breaths and try to forget that until today, I've never even worn a bikini. I'm not sure I still own a bathing suit at all. A T-shirt and shorts work just fine for reading by the pool. Which, come to think of it, is exactly what I'm supposed to be doing during this vacation.

I sneak a peek at my to-be-read pile on the nightstand— which I lovingly refer to as my TBR stack—half expecting to see dust gathering on the book jackets. Poor neglected things.

"Charlotte, you're going to have to face your reflection sooner or later," Ginny says quietly.

Fine.

Reluctantly, I turn my attention toward the mirror and take a good hard look.

She's right. It's not bad. If I ignore my head, I can almost believe I'm looking at Ginny's body instead of mine. But, oh yeah, my face looks exactly like hers too now. I keep forgetting.

"Well?" my twin prompts.

"I haven't felt this naked since the day we were born," I say flatly.

She rolls her eyes. "Dramatic much? Honestly, this bikini isn't overly revealing. The bottoms are high-waisted and the top is substantial enough to fit an actual bra underneath it. It's a pageant swimsuit. Bathing suits that people wear to the beach or even on cruises expose a lot more skin."

Our gazes meet in the mirror, and I quickly look away.

A little over a year ago, Dad and Susan took the whole family on a cruise to celebrate their twentieth wedding anniversary. All three of Susan's kids are married, and she's got a grandchild. Her whole crew was there, and of course so were Ginny and I. Adam and I were already engaged, so he came along, as did Ginny's boyfriend du jour. I can't remember his name. Rick, maybe? Jeremy?

Most of my memories of that cruise involve the sinking feeling I got every time I saw Adam staring at Ginny in her tiny string bikini. I told myself it was no big deal. After all, the swimsuit was indeed microscopic, and Ginny definitely wore it with confidence. He probably couldn't help himself. He was only human.

But weeks after we'd come home and I realized he'd bookmarked her Instagram on his iPad, I began to wonder. It turned out that following her on Instagram was only the tip of the iceberg.

Could I have been any more blind? Or pathetic?

It's in the past.

But it doesn't feel like history. The humiliation is still raw. Fresh. I know I should be over everything that happened, but I'm not. And standing here staring at myself in Ginny's swimsuit feels like pressing a tender bruise.

"I need some air." I yank one of the hotel bathrobes off a hanger in the closet, shove my arms in its sleeves and head for the door.

"Wait. What?" Ginny chases after me. "You can't *leave*. We have loads of work to do. You have to be onstage in less than four hours."

"This is a lot, Ginny. *A lot*. You're used to it. You *chose* it. I didn't. I'll only be gone for a little bit." I grab Buttercup's leash. If I'm going outside, I might as well take the dog with me. Otherwise, I'll just end up having to do it later because I've somehow become responsible for every living creature in this room. All three of us. "Four hours is plenty of time."

I'm sure it's not. No amount of time would prepare me for this.

"But we've got to practice your walk, and your poses, and . . ."

Poses? There are *poses*?

"Ugh, never mind."

I yank the belt of my bathrobe into a tight knot, scoop Buttercup into my arms, and march toward the door.

Ginny is fluttering around me in a panic.

Doesn't she know how hard this is for me?

No, she doesn't. And that's precisely the problem.

"Promise me you're coming back," she blurts, throwing herself between me and the exit.

I'm not sure how she thinks I'm going to permanently

disappear wearing nothing but a bathing suit and a bath-robe. On second thought, I would totally head to the air-port like this if I didn't think it would crush the only dream she's ever had.

I sigh. "I promise."

"Okay." She eyes me warily, then produces her Miss Texas sash from behind her back. "But you can't leave the room without this, remember?"

Somehow, I suppress the very real urge to rip it in two. I let Ginny slip it over my head and one of my arms, so it sits diagonally across my torso. I'm sure it's killing her that I'm leaving the room without being dressed as if I'm walking the runway at Fashion Week, but she seems to know better than to press the point.

If I stay in this room another minute, I will hyper-ventilate.

Or worse.

I'll tell her everything that transpired with Adam, and I can't do that. It wasn't her fault. Of course it wasn't. But she'd feel terrible about it. She'd feel responsible. I know she would.

I can't look her in the eye right now, for fear of spilling my guts. My gaze is fixed on the floor, and I finally see her feet step out of my way. I hold Buttercup tightly against my chest, a barrier of sorts, and walk out the door.

I have no idea where I'm going. I just need to be someplace where I won't be bombarded by anything pageant-related for a few minutes. Someplace where I can just be myself—before I forget who I actually am.

I slip down the stairwell and take Buttercup for a short jaunt around the patch of grass behind the building. Even back here, I'm aware of other pageant girls staring at me with mouths agape. Surprisingly, most of them are dressed casually, in skinny jeans and wedges. But my robe is a standout.

"Come on, Buttercup," I mutter.

The little bulldog follows me back into the building. The jingle in my pockets tells me I've got a few coins on me, which I pour directly into the first floor vending machine. I have enough money to yield three candy bars, and while this seems like an enormous mistake on swimsuit day, I can't help myself. I've hardly eaten since my crazy pageant adventure began.

Pockets loaded down with chocolate, I return to the stairwell, climb to the landing, and collapse into a heap in the corner. Pathetic, I know. But it's the only place where I can escape the nonsense around me.

I lean my head back against the wall, close my eyes, and sit quietly for a minute, relishing the silence. If I try really hard, I can almost pretend I'm back at the library, sitting between the stacks after school, inhaling the comforting scent of ink on paper. But when I take a deep inhale, the stairwell smells dank. Buttercup is like a lead weight in my lap, and within seconds she's snoring loud enough to peel the paint off the walls.

There's no denying where I am.

I open my eyes, pull the candy bars from my pocket, and line them up on the floor beside me. My stomach growls, and its echo drowns out even Buttercup's snores. I'm starving.

Even though I know every other Miss American Treasure contestant in the building is probably noshing on a lettuce leaf or a tiny pile of kale today, I shove all three candy bars into my mouth in quick succession.

I'm not going to lie. For a few minutes, I actually feel better. I'm doing something that Ginny would never, ever do, and it reminds me that I'm still me. I'm still Charlotte. No matter how hard I try or which swimsuit I cram myself into, I'll never, ever, be my twin.

And that's okay.

Deep down, I know it's not a competition. It never was. Not even in those dark days of my engagement.

But my solace is short-lived. I hear footsteps on the stairway above me, and they're accompanied by the unmistakable sound of a snuffling French bulldog.

Him again.

My first instinct is to run and hide. The absolute last thing I need right now is another one-on-one encounter with that man. But it's too late to escape, and besides, a part of me—the foolish part, the *wounded* part—has something to say. Mainly because I'm filled with nonsensical rage at the idea that I can't escape the absurd reality of my situation. Not even for five measly minutes.

And also because, how dare he speak to me like he did yesterday?

How *dare* he?

He reaches the bottom step, rounds the corner of the landing and stops dead in his tracks when he sees me sitting there.

"Fancy meeting you here," I say frostily.

I half expect him to ignore me and walk away without saying a word, but he doesn't. He stares at me for a beat, his expression a perfectly sculpted, unreadable mask. Then his gaze rakes over me, taking in my sash, my bathrobe, the snoring dog in my lap, and then finally, the pile of candy bar wrappers next to me.

For reasons I can't begin to fathom, his mouth curves into a smile.

And despite the fact that I've decided I despise him now, an undeniable flutter courses through me. It's infuriating.

"Something funny?" I ask, depositing Buttercup on the floor and rising to my feet so I can look him in the eyes. They look impossibly blue at such close range. It's like standing beneath a midsummer starry sky.

You know, if you're into that kind of thing.

I swallow. Hard.

"You just never fail to surprise me, Hermione." My heart gives an annoying little leap at the sound of my nickname. "That's all."

It almost sounds like a compliment, but it can't be. Not after yesterday.

"I certainly surprised you in my interview, much to your disappointment." Either Buttercup or Hamlet lets out a timely snort. I'm not sure which. They are mirror images of each other. "You made that clear."

His smile fades. "Are you denying the fact that the things you've told me contradict your questionnaire in almost every way? It's as if it was filled out by another person entirely."

Maybe because it was.

He's right, obviously. But I don't want to hear it. I'm doing the best I can, and he left me feeling as though I'd disappointed him personally. As if I'd let him down.

And I refuse to apologize for the fact that I'm not Ginny.

Only I can't tell him that, can I?

"I get it. You think I'm a liar." I try to force myself to look away from those startling blue eyes but I can't, not even when he responds with a wince.

Followed by a blunt question. "Aren't you?"

I refuse to answer, for obvious reasons. "Are you always so judgmental?"

"*Judgmental?* Are you serious?" He takes a step closer,

until I can feel the heat of his indignation rolling off his muscular form in waves. I find myself leaning into it, like a wildflower basking in the warmth of the sun. I'm not sure why, because I hate him. I really do. "I may be many things, but I assure you that judgmental isn't one of them."

I aim an accusatory glance at the little gold badge pinned to the lapel of his impeccably cut suit. The one that has *Judge* engraved on it in elegant script. "Really? Because judging people is literally your job."

His eyes go dark now—grayish blue, like a storm gathering over the ocean. And the set of his jaw is suddenly so hard it looks like he could cut diamonds with it.

A weighted silence settles between us, but not the calm kind of quiet that I know and love so well. This stillness feels alive. Anticipatory. If it were a color, it would be a deep, glittering red.

He's angry.

I don't care. I'm on a roll, emboldened for reasons only partially related to the man standing in front of me. I've kept too many secrets. I'm full to bursting with them, and he's right here, listening to me as though it matters.

As though *I* matter.

"Do you find it at all creepy that later today you're going to be sitting at the end of a runway judging fifty women on how they look in a swimsuit?" I'm officially losing it. Where has my filter gone?

I've never spoken to anyone so bluntly in my life.

"As a matter of fact, it does make me feel slightly uncomfortable." He arches a brow. "I suppose I *am* a creep. A judgmental one at that. I should probably move into Slytherin and call it a day."

Another Harry Potter reference. A clever one, considering Slytherin is known as the Hogwarts house where all the evil, cunning wizards reside.

I'm both furious and charmed.

And as much as I hate to even think about it, I'm also slightly aroused. Damn him, and damn his sexy, bookish mind.

"I have to go." *Before I do something completely idiotic like kiss you.*

He steps aside for me and Buttercup to pass. The dogs are reluctant to leave each other, locked in a playful somersault and grunting with joy. I manage to drag Buttercup away, but just as we're about to step out of reach, Hamlet's dad gives the belt of my robe a gentle tug.

His voice goes soft, but there's an edge to it that scrapes my insides and makes me ache. "No one is forcing you to do this, Hermione. Remember that."

Actually . . .

I take a shuddering inhale and force a beauty queen smile. "You're absolutely right."

9

Just under four hours later, I'm standing backstage with forty-nine other girls who, like me, are wearing nothing but half a yard of Lycra swimwear, their state sash, and enough adhesive spray to permanently destroy the ozone layer.

The aerosol adhesive is a pageant trick, apparently, and it's kind of miraculous. Ginny sprayed it liberally on my rear end so my swimsuit bottoms wouldn't ride up when I walk.

Correction: glide.

I'm supposed to glide like Kate Middleton when I cross the stage. No walking allowed, because I've apparently been doing it wrong for the past twenty-nine years. Ginny schooled me in the pageant walk all afternoon. I'm a hopeless cause. And even though I never managed to cross the length of our hotel room without tripping, she held my glasses hostage and refused to let me put them on.

This is going to be a complete and utter disaster. I'm dreading every minute of it, partly because I'm still fuming over my stairway encounter with Judge Fitzwilliam Darcy and partly because I've never been quite this naked in public.

There must be solidarity in numbers, though, because I feel much less conspicuous now that I'm here with the other girls. I mean, we're all basically in the same cringe-worthy position. Even though the amount of body fat in the room is probably too microscopic to measure, all of us have the same expression on our faces. It's a cross between a deer caught in the headlights and Wonder Woman preparing to smash the patriarchy.

We're brimming with confidence. After all, forty-nine of us have been preparing for this moment for months. Yet at the same time, there isn't a single contestant who isn't sneaking anxious glances at the full-length mirrors that are strategically placed in the four corners of the backstage area.

I'm searching for Miss Nevada somewhere among the sea of flat stomachs and spray tans that are just shy of tan-orexic when a woman in a black T-shirt emblazoned with the Miss American Treasure logo blocks my path.

"Where are you going?" She points somewhere behind me. "Miss Texas is supposed to be over there, between Tennessee and Utah. It's all alphabetical. We went over this at rehearsal, remember?"

I grit my teeth. No, I don't remember, because rehearsal was held two days ago, before Ginny's allergy attack. "Got it."

But she must not believe me because she escorts me to the proper place, inserts me between Miss Tennessee and Miss Utah, and makes me swear to stay put. I obey.

Surprisingly, I'm not at all tempted to flee. I need to do this. Not just for Ginny, but also for me. I need to prove to that arrogant Gray Beckham that he hasn't gotten under my skin.

He has, in a major way. But no one else needs to know that, especially him.

I'm not even sure why he's gotten me so stirred up. I just know that I find him infuriating, and I suddenly want to rock my bikini in a way that will make him sorry he stifled a laugh when he found me surrounded by candy bar wrappers in the stairwell.

At the memory of my vending machine haul, my stomach growls so loud that I can hear it above the din of the chaos backstage. I don't regret a single nibble. In spite of all her talk about body positivity, Ginny declared food off-limits until the swimsuit prelims are over tonight. She's promised me the dinner of my dreams, and in the meantime, I'm once again starving.

Clearly, I'm not the only one.

"I'm having a pizza the minute this is over," Miss Tennessee says. "An entire pie, all to myself."

Miss Utah laughs. "Oh my God, me too. Followed by a banana split."

"I was seriously tempted earlier by the bag of puppy chow in my room," I say drily. I'm only half joking, by the way.

The contestants around me laugh, and Miss Tennessee murmurs under her breath. "I'm sharing a room with Miss Virginia, and we're having a cheeseburger party right after this—fries, onion rings, the works. You should stop by. Just don't tell the pageant officials."

My mouth falls open. "Why? Are burgers actually *illegal*?"

"No, but we want to keep it casual. No selfies, no Instagrams, no tweets. We want to hang out in sweatpants and be ourselves for a little while, you know?"

I *do* know. And frankly, as much as I love my twin, a little time apart might do us some good. That hotel room is feeling a little crowded. "That sounds perfect. I'm in."

Seconds later, the production assistant is back, giving us some final words of wisdom.

"Don't forget that you're supposed to walk onstage when the announcer introduces the girl in front of you. Enter from stage left and walk to the center of the stage. There's an *X* made out of yellow tape on the floor, marking your spot. Once you hit it, strike your pose and hold it while the other girl does her runway walk. Understood?"

We all nod.

"After the girl before you makes her exit, the announcer will call your state and you've got ninety seconds to walk the runway. Make the most of it! Take your time. Don't rush, and most of all, remember to pause and make eye contact with each of the judges."

Oh boy.

I have to make eye contact with my nemesis . . . while wearing a bikini.

My stomach lurches. Maybe those candy bars weren't such a brilliant idea after all.

You can do this, Snickers be damned.

The producer leaves, and Miss Tennessee, Miss Utah, and I all look at one another.

"We're ready for this," Miss Tennessee says resolutely. "Both of you look amazing."

"So do you," I say.

Miss Utah nods in agreement, takes both of our hands in hers and gives them a tight squeeze. "We've got this. We're beautiful women, inside and out."

I return her hand squeeze and my throat clogs.

What is happening to me? I can't possibly be getting choked up over a swimsuit competition in a beauty pageant. Competing in this thing has got to be the absolute dumbest thing I've ever done. I should be crying tears of shame.

But the pep talk throws me off-kilter. Of course Ginny

told me I look great and assured me I can rock this if I remember to slow down and "embrace my authenticity," whatever that means.

She has to say those things, though. She's my twin, and after all, I'm doing this for her.

Miss Tennessee and Miss Utah, not so much. They're my competition, and yet both women seem so genuinely supportive. I'm not sure why I'm surprised. Miss Nevada has been nothing but kind to me, too. Growing up with Ginny exposed me to about a million pageants on television, and when the winner is announced, she's always mobbed by sobbing girls who act as if they're almost as happy for her as they are sad for themselves. I guess I just always thought it was an act.

Maybe it's not. Maybe these women really do all get along.

For the most part, anyway. I'm sure there are a few mean girls in the bunch. Aren't there always?

I haven't encountered any yet, though. Weirdly enough, it's starting to feel like a sisterhood. Even stranger, I almost feel like I belong.

"Welcome to the preliminary swimsuit competition of the Miss American Treasure pageant!" The announcer's voice booms throughout the ballroom, and my mouth goes dry as a bone.

This is really happening.

All the pageant prelims are taking place in the ballroom, the same room where we had our interviews yesterday. But the space looks nothing like it did the day before. An elevated stage has been constructed along the far wall, with a long runway extending about two-thirds the length of the room. The judging panel sits at a long table running parallel to the runway, extremely close. The whole eye contact thing is going to be a challenge at such close range.

Those of us hailing from states in the second half of the alphabet cluster together in the wings, watching the action onstage as the A through D states strut their stuff. It's not at all what I expect.

Watching a pageant in person is a completely different experience from sitting in your living room and watching it on television. It feels almost intimate.

It's immediately obvious which contestants are nervous and which ones feel at ease. Like Ginny said, the girls who are flustered hurry down the runway, barely pausing to pose. Some of them seem to focus on the judges' foreheads rather than looking them square in the eye. Their arms are stiff. Some of them scrunch their shoulders. I swear, Miss Connecticut has the body of a Victoria's Secret model, but she walks across the stage with actual jazz hands.

Jazz hands.

Ginny was right. This spectacle isn't really about bodies. Not altogether, anyway. It's about body confidence. I never would have believed it if I didn't have what basically amounts to a front-row seat.

This epiphany should really make me feel better. Unfortunately, my walk isn't any better than my bikini body. Truth be told, it's probably worse. So now I'm not only worried about the slight jiggle in my belly and getting down the runway and back without falling on my face, but I'm also concerned about my shoulders, my arms, the stiffness of my smile, and the possibility that I might have a hidden propensity for jazz hands.

I swallow and make fists at my sides—a preemptive measure. Then another pageant official wearing a Miss American Treasure jacket and wielding a clipboard arrives to herd us back into position.

"Back in line, girls. We're already halfway through the alphabet." She waves her arms at us as if we're cattle, and I can't really fault her, because the clomp of our platform stilettos against the stage floor does sound rather cowlike.

Great, another thing for me to worry about when it's my turn. Which will be here any second, because time is suddenly moving at warp speed. We fly through the *O*'s, and when Miss Rhode Island takes the stage and strikes her pose behind Miss Pennsylvania, I'm struck with the realization that there are only three more girls standing between me and my onstage pageant debut.

Oh God.

I close my eyes and try to "find my center," as Ginny and her yoga-loving friends always say. But I'm so jittery right now that I'm not sure I actually have a center. I am a doughnut.

I'm also a fraud.

I'm nothing but a big, fraudulent doughnut.

And now I'm hungry again. The sudden roar of applause drags me away from thoughts of Krispy Kreme and back to my doughnut-free reality. All the women around me are clapping and cheering. Beside me, Miss Tennessee is waving her hands frantically in front of her face to ward off tears.

Intrigued by all the hoopla, I crane my neck for a better glimpse of the runway. What could possibly be going on out there? I'm almost expecting to see a beauty queen equivalent of Gisele Bündchen gliding up and down the catwalk, but I don't. What I actually see is even better.

Miss South Carolina is in the center of the runway, smiling down at the judges. Like nearly all the other contestants, she's wearing a bikini, which means her abdomen is on display for everyone to see. To my complete and utter surprise, there's a large scar running down the center of her torso. It starts at her sternum and runs almost all the way down to her belly button.

I can't believe I didn't notice it when she was standing backstage, awaiting her turn with the rest of us. But it's pretty dark back here, and until the competition began, I was too consumed with checking out my own body in the mirror to notice anyone but the girls standing on either side of me.

Right now, though, I can't tear my eyes off of Miss South Carolina. Her smile is electric. Every step she takes radiates poise and grace. Watching her gives me goose bumps. It's *that* powerful.

"I heard she had open-heart surgery less than a year ago," Miss Utah whispers. "She's got some kind of rare cardiac disorder. As Miss South Carolina, she visits a lot of hospitals."

Now I'm the one on the verge of tears. I blink furiously. She could have easily chosen a one-piece swimsuit, but she didn't. She's out there owning her scar.

Watching her prance and twirl isn't just inspiring. It's empowering, just like Ginny said. I'm brimming with admiration.

Oh no, I've sipped the Kool-Aid.

I sigh inwardly. Of course I haven't. I'm just a placeholder. I'm not even competing in this thing. Not for real.

But when it's my turn to walk onstage, it certainly feels real. The dazzling set is real and so is the surge of adrenaline that hits my veins when the announcer calls my name and the warmth of the spotlight turns toward me.

Oh my God. Oh my God. Oh my God.

I'm doing it. I'm walking the runway, and it's not nearly

as scary as I thought it would be. Every time a worrisome thought about my appearance enters my head, I think about Miss South Carolina. If she can do this, I can too.

Music is playing over the loudspeakers. It's a song by someone named Zayn or Justin or Harry that I've heard the tween girls go crazy for at the karaoke booth at my school's fall festival. The beat's familiarity gives me a little boost and, miraculously, I realize I'm moving with what I think is known as swagger.

My head spins. I'm actually—dare I say it—enjoying myself. Almost. I'm still playing a part, only this time I'm the one cast as Miss Texas. Not my twin. Not Ginny.

Me.

I reach the middle of the runway, and I pause to stand with my hands on my hips and my head tilted just so, exactly like Ginny taught me to do. One by one, I look each judge in the eye. They're seated in the same order as they were yesterday during the interviews, and each one of them smiles back at me.

Until I get to the end.

Him.

Again.

His gaze is impassive. Stoic. And it never wavers from my face, as if he's dead set on ignoring the fact that I'm standing there in a bathing suit that could probably pass for a push-up bra and panties.

Look at me, damn it.

I do a little spin, then arch a brow. It's a challenge, and we both know it. I'm daring him to look. It's his job, after all. He's here to judge me in all my bikini'd glory. He can't just ignore me and refuse to venture a glance below my neck.

But that's obviously his intention.

He's getting me back for calling him creepy. Fine. Two can play at that game. If he wants to ignore me, I'll ignore him right back.

I keep moving—past the judges' table and all the way to the end of the runway, where I do the pose, turn, pose combination that Ginny made me practice for half an hour. I'm not completely sure I get it right, but close enough. I'm not sprinting offstage, and there's not a jazz hand in sight.

On my way back toward the stage, I pass the judges' table again and flash judges one through five each another grin. When my handsome, book-quoting nemesis comes into view, I pretend he's wearing Harry Potter's invisibility cloak. I look right through him.

When I'm back at the top of the stage and my ninety seconds are nearly up, I give one last hair toss and cast a demure glance over my shoulder. Then, and only then, do I catch my Slytherin friend watching me.

I do something I know I shouldn't.

I wink at him.

He drops his gaze immediately, focusing on the binder spread open in front of him. Once again, he's all business as he jots something down in his judge's book, but I'm almost certain I spy a tiny hitch in the corner of his lips. The barest hint of a smile.

Or maybe it's just wishful thinking.

10

*G*inny isn't crazy about the whole cheeseburger-party thing.

"I thought we could order some room service together and watch a movie. You know, Netflix and chill." She frowns as she catches my gaze in the reflection of the bathroom mirror where she's busy putting a deep-conditioning mask on her hair.

I know I've been out of the dating scene for a while, but I'm pretty sure Netflix and chill means something else. Still, I refrain from correcting her, lest it lead to another conversation about my relationship status.

"We will when I get back. I promise." I flip open my suitcase and pull out my favorite sweatpants. "I won't stay long, but I think I should at least make an appearance. Don't you? Won't it be weird if I keep staying holed up in here? Don't you usually socialize with the other contestants?"

Ginny sighs. "I guess. I'm just getting a little bored. I think I'm stir-crazy from hiding in this room, you know?"

As a matter of fact, I *do* know. The Huntington Spa Resort is a nice place and all, but being trapped in here with my twin is beginning to feel like a bedazzled prison sentence. Every time I turn around, Ginny's coming at me with a brush or an eyelash curler or lip liner. The sheets on my bed are stained from self-tanner, so it looks like I've been rolling around in Cheeto dust every night before hitting the hay. I barely recognize my own reflection in the mirror, and I can't remember the last time I cracked a book.

I need some space.

A cheeseburger party in yet another hotel room isn't exactly an escape, but it's as close as I'm going to get until the pageant is over. "I'll stay for an hour or less, and then I'll come right back. Deal?"

"Fine." Ginny snaps a shower cap over her hair mask and leans closer to the mirror to inspect her face. The swelling has gone down quite a bit, but she's still not even close to being back in beauty queen form. Her complexion is covered in red splotches and she looks weirdly out of proportion, almost like a Picasso painting. Her cheeks seem normal-size but her lips are still comically huge and one eye is bigger than the other.

It's been nearly forty-eight hours since our visit to the urgent-care clinic. The doctor told her she'd be back to normal in three if she was lucky, and Ginny's always been lucky. Her life is definitely charmed. We both thought she'd be ready to compete by tomorrow.

Neither of us mention that now, though. I'm sure Ginny is still holding on to hope, and I don't want to upset her. Besides, maybe she'll wake up tomorrow and miraculously look like herself again. God, I hope so. The talent preliminaries are tomorrow. I managed to survive the interviews and actually did okay in the swimsuit competition, but talent is another matter entirely.

"You can't go like that, though." Ginny spins around to aim a disgusted glance at my Hogwarts T-shirt and sweats. "No way."

"Yes, I can. It's casual. Torrie specifically said to wear sweatpants." I gather my hair, plus the five pounds of extensions attached to it, into a messy bun.

Ginny pulls an alternate sweatshirt out of her closet and shoves it toward me. It's pink. Because of course it is.

"Who's Torrie, again?" she asks.

"Miss Tennessee. She seems really nice." I snatch the sweatshirt from her hands and glare at it. "Is this really necessary? It's a cheeseburger party."

"I know, but you're supposed to be me. And right now you look a little too much like . . ."

"Like myself?" I snap.

She blinks, and in an instant her expression changes

135

from annoyed to hurt. "Well, that is the whole point of taking my place. Remember?"

Right. How could I forget? For days, I haven't been allowed to wear my own clothes, use my own name, or in any way act like myself.

"Sorry," I mutter. "I'll wear the sweatshirt."

I shut myself in the bathroom to pull it on, not so much for modesty reasons but because I feel like I might cry all of a sudden.

I felt so good after the swimsuit competition. As cheesy as it sounds, I was proud. But now I'm being reminded once again that I'm not actually good enough to be here. Taking Ginny's place is supposed to be a *privilege*, not just a favor.

Why should I miss being Charlotte?

"You might want to rethink the messy bun too," Ginny says through the door.

I fling it open. "The bun stays."

"It could damage your extensions," she counters.

"That's a risk I'm willing to take," I say hotly.

We're bickering like we did when we were teenagers, but I don't care. She's getting on my last nerve.

I grab a room key and tuck it into the kangaroo pocket of Ginny's pink sweatshirt. Have I mentioned the sweatshirt is cashmere? Who wears *cashmere* sweats?

Beauty queens, apparently. And as much as I hate to admit it, the sweatshirt is super comfy. Maybe even the softest thing I've ever worn, damn it.

Couldn't she be wrong about something? Just once?

"I'll be back in an hour or less," I say, pausing by the door.

Ginny ignores me because it seems we're fighting now, which is exactly what I was trying to avoid by escaping for a little while. Perfect.

I slip the Miss Texas sash over my head. Ginny watches me in the reflection of the mirror, but says nothing. I can tell watching me take her place is more painful than she realized it would be.

But it was her idea, not mine. I didn't want any of this. I have nothing to feel guilty about.

Then why do you?

I push this question as far from my thoughts as I can while I make my way to Torrie's room. I know I've got the right one when I hear music and laughter streaming into the hallway. I knock three times, and the door swings open almost immediately, revealing Torrie and about eight to ten other contestants.

Girls are sitting on both beds, the love seat, and the floor, and to my immense delight, they're all wearing actual sweatpants. Some are even in their pajamas. If not for the glam hair, lashes, and extreme tans, they'd look like any normal bunch of friends getting together for a night in.

"You probably want to take that off." Torrie gestures to my Miss Texas sash. "At my last pageant, a girl got honey mustard on hers and it wouldn't come out. She legit had to compete in the evening gown competition with a yellow stain covering one of her state letters."

My jaw falls open in horror, mainly because if such a terrifying thing happened to anyone in this room, it would no doubt be me.

"Note taken." I slip the sash over my head and drape it over a hanger in the open closet, where all the other guests at this little shindig have discarded theirs. A quarter of the country is represented, from New York to California. It's like a sparkly Congress.

"Everyone, this is Ginny Gorman from Texas," Torrie says, waving at me with a flourish, Vanna White–style.

I'm welcomed with a chorus of hellos. Torrie's roommate, Miss Virginia, introduces herself and I take a seat on the floor, crisscross applesauce.

"Didn't we compete together once?" A willowy brunette narrows her gaze at me over an onion ring.

The servings are small. Miniscule, actually. Each burger is cut into quarters and we're all sharing single orders of fries and onion rings, but I don't care. It's food. At this point, I'd happily gnaw on one of the paper napkins.

"I think we did. What was it? Miss . . ." I grab a handful of fries and shove them into my mouth, buying time.

"Miss American Daydream," she says. "I'm sure that was it."

Thank goodness. I nod and reach for a section of cheeseburger. The food tastes so good I'm afraid I might start drooling all over myself.

"So how did it go for everyone today? Any horror stories?" Torrie plops down beside me on the carpet and then slides the basket of fries between us. She's definitely my new best friend.

"When I came out of the ballroom, my pageant coach told me that the double-sided tape on my swimsuit top was showing," a blonde stretched out on one of the beds says. "I wanted to die."

"If that's the worst thing that happens to you during this pageant, I think you're safe," someone says.

I nod. "Agreed. I wet my pants in my first pageant."

The room goes silent.

"I was four years old," I add.

Torrie bursts into laughter, and everyone else follows.

"Oh my God, you're hilarious. Thanks for that. I needed a good laugh," the blonde says.

One by one, we bemoan the struggles we've experienced thus far throughout the preliminaries. The tales are an assortment of self-tanning mishaps, lost earrings, and broken stilettos. One poor girl had a strip of false eyelashes fall off during her personal interview.

"It started coming loose, and then it just slid down my face like a black fuzzy caterpillar." She sighs.

Torrie and I exchange a mortified glance, and then she says, "What did you do?"

"I left it there until my three minutes was up. I figured acknowledging it would just draw attention to it. Was that the wrong call?"

There's a beat of silence, during which we all conjure a mental picture of an eyelash caterpillar crawling down her face. A snicker escapes me. I can't help it. Within seconds, the entire party collapses into a fit of giggles.

For the first time in days, I actually let myself relax. I'm having fun. I remind myself that I'm supposed to be Ginny, not Charlotte. But as the evening progresses, I let my guard down just a little bit.

The conversation turns to the judges. Torrie thinks the former *Bachelorette* contestant is hot, and I let my opinion fly.

"I don't know," I say. "I think it's gross that he's judging a pageant. He's a man. It just seems a little archaic."

The girl on the other side of Torrie snorts. "More archaic than anything *Bachelor* related?"

Point taken.

"Okay, so maybe it's on-brand for him. But what about the other man on the panel? What's his excuse?" I roll my eyes.

Rein it in.

I shouldn't be drawing any attention whatsoever to Gray. But thoughts of him have been flitting around my consciousness all day, and now I've gone and done it.

My cheeks burn and I drop my gaze, focusing intently on the tiny pile of fries on the paper plate in my lap.

"You mean Gray Beckham?"

I shrug, feigning nonchalance as best as I can. "I think that's his name."

"Judge number six?" The willowy brunette is the first to speak up. "Yep, that's it. He owns the Miss Starlight pageant."

"What?" I gape at her. "He *owns* a beauty pageant?"

The food in my stomach curdles into a sickening ball of grease and cheese. I feel sick.

Torrie nods. "Yes, he started it a few years ago."

A shudder crawls up my spine. How could I have misjudged someone so much? He started his own *pageant?* I mean, how does that even happen? Was he just sitting around one day and decided he needed a bunch of beautiful women parading around purely for his enjoyment? Does he have some sort of Hugh Hefner complex? What makes a man start a business just so he can rank women in order of his preference?

This is worse than *The Bachelor*. Way worse. It's even worse than *Bachelor in Paradise*, which Ginny made me watch once on her birthday. Trust me, it was like witnessing a reality show that had been filmed in a fraternity house during Rush Week. Gray Beckham and his depraved entrepreneurial spirit actually makes the entire Bachelor franchise seem quaint and wholesome by comparison.

Ew. Double ew.

Ew times infinity.

"That's the most perverted thing I've ever heard," I blurt.

I can't believe I wasted even a second of my precious time feeling guilty about what I said to him earlier. And to think he tried to say he felt uncomfortable judging the swimsuit competition.

Who's the liar now?

"Don't any of you agree?" I glance around the room, searching for partners in my outrage, but no one says a word. Some of the women are frowning, and others seem to be trying not to look at me.

"Come on, y'all. It's creepy. You have to admit," I say.

Torrie clears her throat. "Um, Ginny? You're familiar with the Miss Starlight pageant, right?"

I'm not.

"Sure." I shrug.

Something in Torrie's perfect cat eyes tells me I've just screwed up. Big time.

She clears her throat and speaks her next words with an exaggerated calm. "Then you know that it's the charity supported by the Miss American Treasure organization, kind of like how the Miss America pageant supports the Make-A-Wish foundation."

I blink. I'm still not sure where she's going with this, but it can't be good.

"It's a pageant for little girls who are terminally ill," she says flatly.

"Every girl gets a crown," Miss Georgia, sitting on the other side of me, adds. "Every girl gets applauded and celebrated and told how special and beautiful she is."

"Oh," I manage to sputter. I try to swallow but my throat goes dry. "I didn't realize . . ."

Every eye in the room is fixed on me.

"Seriously? You didn't know?" The girl with the wandering caterpillar lashes sits up straighter on the bed, studying me. "How is that possible? It was all over our pageant welcome packet. Every one of us had to sign a pledge promising to act as emcee for the next Miss Starlight pageant in the event we're crowned Miss American Treasure. The top ten finalists all show up every year to pose for pictures with the little girls and help the ones in wheelchairs get down the runway."

Wow.

I try to imagine such a pageant, and I can't. It's too poignant. Too devastating. If I think too hard about sick little girls in tiaras, I'll start sobbing. It sounds so . . .

So sweet. And heartbreaking. And not creepy in the slightest.

Quite the opposite, actually. The Miss Starlight pageant seems like a wonderful thing. A kind, compassionate thing.

Which would make the man who created it more of a real-life Prince Charming than the supervillain I've made him out to be.

Oh my God, what have I done?

My paper plate slips out of my hands, falling onto the carpet with a plop. It echoes throughout the quiet room.

I've accused a perfectly nice man—an *honorable* man who does things like make terminally ill children feel special and beautiful—of wanting to do nothing but ogle women in bikinis. I told him to his face that I think he's pervy.

Why didn't he say anything?

He could have berated me right there in the stairwell. He probably could have reported me to the pageant officials and told them I was unfit to wear the crown. Because clearly I'm not worthy.

He didn't do any of those things, though. Instead, he'd just looked at me with that brooding glint in his moody blue eyes and tried to make light of my scathing assessment of him.

"I've made a terrible mistake," I whisper. My voice cracks, which seems appropriate, since I suddenly feel like I'm coming apart at the seams.

"Don't beat yourself up about it. You didn't know. You probably just got the name of the pageant confused with another one." Torrie gives my leg a pat.

"Yeah." The willowy brunette nods. "Who can keep up with all the various titles? I need a spreadsheet just to plan my year. I'm at a different pageant almost every weekend."

"Spoken like a true crown chaser," Miss Virginia says.

Everyone laughs.

Everyone but me, that is.

I try to swallow. I can't eat anymore—my throat is too thick with regret.

And shame. No wonder Gray Beckham refused to look at me during the swimsuit competition. He probably loathes the very sight of me.

I take a shuddering breath.

But he *had* looked, hadn't he? He'd stared right at me when he thought I wouldn't notice.

At least I think he did. Now I'm not so sure.

11

As soon as I can manage, I excuse myself from the hotel room party and take shelter in the stairwell. The minute I'm alone, I pull out my phone.

I've got a few texts from Ginny, plus one missed call, but I ignore those and tap the little internet browser icon. I'm desperate for information on a certain pageant judge, and Google is my friend.

Within seconds, I'm on the Miss Starlight website, looking at pictures of smiling, delicate little girls with sparkling tiaras on their tiny heads, dressed in enough tulle to choke a Disney princess. I flip past photo after photo, with tears streaming down my face. I can't bear to look, but I also can't make myself put down my phone.

These little girls are brave. Special. They deserve to be celebrated . . . to be seen.

If anyone knows the value of such appreciation, it's me.

I choke on a sob, but I keep scrolling. I take in every

last picture, every glittering crown, every triumphant grin until I finally reach the end. The girls range from age five all the way up to the late teens. Some of them are bald from chemo treatments. Others walk down the runway pulling their IV poles alongside them.

Each and every one of them is beautiful.

Any of these girls could have been students at my school—kids I interact with every day, kids I care about. I wonder how many of them have passed away since they moved across that stage.

My heart beats hard in my chest. I'm afraid to know the answer.

I give into the weakness in my knees and sink down onto one of the steps. I scroll to the top of the website and click on a tab labeled *History of the Miss Starlight pageant.*

My hands tremble violently as I read the truth about Gray Beckham.

The Miss Starlight pageant began in 2010, under the direction of tech billionaire Gray Beckham. Mr. Beckham, a graduate of Harvard with a double degree in computer science and English literature, founded Miss Starlight in loving memory of his sister, Sonja Beckham.

Crowned Miss American Treasure when she was twenty-two years old, Sonja Beckham went on to study medicine at Vanderbilt University Medical Center and worked as a pediatric oncologist at MD Anderson Cancer Center in Houston,

Texas. She was diagnosed with acute myelogenous leukemia in 2009 and passed away six months later at the age of thirty-two.

The Miss Starlight pageant celebrates the life and work of Dr. Beckham and is devoted to celebrating young patients who have been diagnosed with a terminal illness by shining a light on inner beauty and honoring who they are in front of family, friends, and loving supporters.

I sit staring at my phone until it goes dark.

A million thoughts are spinning in my head. First and foremost, I hate cancer. I hate it so hard. It took my mom from me, before I ever really had a chance to know her. It took Gray's sister. But look at him—he's turning his family's pain into something positive and beautiful for the very kids his sister devoted her life to helping.

And in my ignorance, I mocked him for it.

I feel ill.

How could I have made such a damning assumption about a man I didn't even know? A man whom I *liked?*

I keep hoping that if I wait here long enough, he'll show up. I'm not sure what I'll say if he does though. *I'm sorry* seems inadequate.

But it's a start, right?

Minutes pass, and a few times I manage to convince myself that I hear the jingle of Hamlet's dog tag echoing in the concrete stairwell. It's never him, though. It's just me, wiping my wet, tear-stained face with the sleeve of Ginny's posh cashmere sweatshirt.

When I'm finally ready to face the outside world again, I get up and slip back into the hallway. The party is still going strong, if the sounds coming from Torrie's room are any indication.

Good for them, I think.

My major faux pas from earlier seems to have blown over. I doubt anyone is suspicious enough to believe that I'm actually a librarian posing as her beauty queen twin, and if I knocked on the door, I'm sure they'd welcome me back into the fold.

I'm not feeling it, though.

I don't want to be Ginny right now. The trouble is, I don't want to be Charlotte either.

The room is dark when I let myself back into it with my card key, which seems odd. It's only eight fifteen, far too early for bed.

"Ginny?" I whisper.

There's no response, other than a snort that sounds more French bulldogish than it does human, so I tiptoe to the bathroom as quietly as I can and flip on the vanity light.

My plan is to strip down, take a hot shower and climb into bed. I just want to wash this horrible day away, but the vanity light casts a soft glow over the room and I catch a glimpse of something unfamiliar on the desk behind me.

I turn around and sigh.

When I left for the cheeseburger party, every available surface in our hotel room was covered with tools of the beauty queen trade—makeup brushes, contour and highlighting powders, hair spray, lashes, and every kind of sparkle imaginable.

But glam central has been cleared away, and now the desk is covered with room service trays. There's a big bowl of spaghetti and meatballs—my favorite—plus two fat slices of chocolate cake. Twin glasses of milk sit in pools of condensation. The spread has been there for a while, it seems.

"I wanted to surprise you with all your favorites," Ginny says in the darkness. "You said you'd be back within an hour."

After the revelation of Gray Beckham's identity, I'd forgotten my promise to my sister. Is there *anything* I'm not going to screw up today?

Buttercup wiggles out from under the covers on Ginny's bed and scurries toward me, wagging her stumpy little tail in glee. I can hardly believe my eyes. It's a breakthrough. She's finally decided I'm tolerable. She might actually *like* me now.

But it's the worst possible time for the dog to have a change of heart. Ginny's brow crumples as Buttercup flops onto her back at my feet.

The bulldog's sudden and over-the-top adoration nearly kills me. I don't deserve it. Not today. "I'm so sorry, Ginny. I screwed up. I . . ."

"You made new friends." She sniffs. "I get it. You were having fun, and you forgot we had plans."

She's only partially right.

I *was* having fun without her, and I'm also guilty of ignoring her texts and calls. It's not the entire story, though.

I want to explain things to my twin. I want to confess. No one understands me the way that Ginny does. Even though the entire episode was my fault, she'd still find a way to make me feel better about it. She'd tell me there was no way I could have known what kind of man Gray Beckham actually is.

She'd take my side, just like always.

But I can't tell her. Too much has happened. I'm in too deep, and trying to unravel the mess I've made would shine a bright, glaring light on all the things I've been keeping from her the past few days.

"Please forgive me." I scoop Buttercup into my arms and sit down on the edge of Ginny's bed. "I'm sorry. Truly."

She shuts her eyes again, but I don't budge.

I'll sit there all night if I have to. I can't go to bed until I make things right with at least one of the people I've hurt.

Don't get me wrong. I know Ginny isn't perfect. She's said plenty of things to me in the past few days that have stung. But she's my sister. My twin. I've never loved anyone the way I love Ginny. And even though I sometimes wonder what my life would have been like if she wasn't my other half—if I hadn't been a twin at all, but just a regular person, just me—I'd never change the way things are.

I give her a gentle poke. "Please? You're the reason I'm in this pageant in the first place, remember? I'd much rather be spending my time reading by the pool." Or better yet, with my head buried under the covers so I'd never have to see any of these pageant people again.

"Fiiiine." She drags her eyes open. "I forgive you. Happy now?"

My gaze flits to the chocolate cake. "Not yet, but I will be once we clean those plates. And don't try to tell me you're not hungry. I haven't seen you eat a full meal in two days."

"That's because I'm scared to eat." She waves a hand at her face. "Look what happened last time I feasted on room service."

"You can't starve yourself, Ginny. The pageant isn't worth your health. Nothing is." I give her a little nudge with my hip. "We could always go home, you know. It's not too late. We could leave tonight if you want. You could see an allergy doctor tomorrow, and then you wouldn't have to worry anymore."

It would all be over . . .

Including Ginny's dream of being Miss American Treasure.

"No." Finally, she sits up. I haven't managed to talk her

out of this painful charade, but at least I've stirred her back to life. "We're so close. I can't give up now."

I nod. "It's your call."

She presses her fingertips gently against her cheeks. "How does my face look? Any better?"

"A little bit." I smile. "Let's not worry about that now. We've got almost twenty hours until talent prelims tomorrow. Anything could happen."

Ginny nods. "You're right."

My smile widens. "I know I am."

She rolls her eyes and pelts me with her pillow. I breathe a sigh of relief. My twin has forgiven me, and everything between us is back to normal.

For now.

We wake up the next morning to chocolate icing in our hair and the sobering realization that Ginny's face doesn't look any different than it did the night before.

"I don't get it." She peers closer to the mirror to inspect her reflection. "Last night I thought I was getting better."

So did I. "Do you want me to take you back to the urgent-care clinic?"

"There's no time. The talent prelims start at three o'clock." She pulls a face. "And, well . . ."

I finish for her. "I have no talent."

Ginny holds up her hands. "You said it. Not me."

"There's got to be something I can do. I'm not audition-ing for the Metropolitan Opera. It's a beauty pageant."

Ginny clears her throat. "Scholarship competition."

I hold up a hand. "Don't start. Please"

Not when I somehow have to learn ventriloquism or how to dance the hula or sing a Bible hymn while signing it in ASL in a mere handful of hours.

I gasp, struck with sudden inspiration. "What about a dramatic reading?"

I've been reading since I was four years old. It's my thing. I wouldn't even need to prepare. Off the top of my head, I can recite half a dozen monologues, from *Romeo and Juliet* to *Macbeth* to *Hamlet*.

I swallow.

The thought of *Hamlet* sends my heart tumbling. I've been doing my best to push Gray Beckham and his altru-istic charms from my mind altogether. It's been hard. So. Very. Hard.

But I can't deal with that humiliating situation at the moment. There are more pressing matters at hand. Besides, I've been taking Buttercup outside as often as I possibly can without causing suspicion, and I haven't seen Gray or his cute little dog at all. It's as if they've packed up and moved out of the Huntington altogether.

Or more likely, Gray is going to great lengths to avoid me.

"A dramatic reading? You're joking, right?" Ginny cringes. The gesture is so exaggerated that she looks more like an emoji than an actual person.

"Why do I get the feeling you think that's a bad idea?"

"Because it is. Contestants only do dramatic readings when they're not capable of doing anything else. As far as talent goes, it's a last resort." She eyes me up and down. "Dead last."

Her comment doesn't even bother me. It's amazing how accustomed I've become to being insulted, all for the sake of a crown.

"What were you planning on doing for talent?"

Ginny has toyed with contemporary dance, traditional flamenco, and classical flute, among other talents. Unlike me, Ginny is blessed in the charisma department. She can get away with pretty much anything onstage.

"I was going to twirl," she says.

This is unexpected. To my knowledge, her long list of competitive talent numbers has never included baton. "I didn't realize you knew how to do that."

"I've been taking lessons for the past six months." Her gaze flits to the picture of our mother, still propped up in a place of honor on Ginny's nightstand. "It's what Mom did when she won."

"That's nice. It's really sweet, sis." I take a deep breath. "Teach me your routine."

She lifts a brow. "Did you not hear what I just said? I've been taking lessons for six months. *Six.* That's half a year."

"I'm familiar with the concept of a calendar." I sigh. "But as you've so bluntly pointed out, I can't do anything else. We've got hours. Why don't you at least try and teach me? Who knows? Maybe I'll catch on freakishly quick."

Maybe if I think of it as an extra-large wand I'll be okay. Not to brag, but I was pretty good with the interactive plastic wand I bought in Diagon Alley at Harry Potter World. I was casting spells all over the place with that thing.

I nod toward Mom's photograph. "It's in the genes. I could be a prodigy. We'll never know unless we try."

Spoiler alert: I'm not a baton-twirling prodigy.

Ginny starts out by teaching me how to do a basic horizontal figure eight.

"Toe under, head on top. Toe under, head on top," she chants, over and over and over again.

The end of the baton slams into my temple with a thud. "Ouch."

"How do you even do that? The baton shouldn't be anywhere near your head right now." She takes hold of my wrist and pulls my arm out straight. "Try again. Toe under, head on top."

My hand goes still and the baton stops moving, midair. "Why do you keep saying that? I don't know what it means."

Ginny takes the baton and points to the white rubber stopper-looking thing at the end. "This is the head. The other end is called the toe."

Sounds simple enough. "How do you tell them apart?"

"The head is larger. Got it?"

I nod. But when I try the figure-eight move again, the head of the baton somehow ends up wedged in my armpit.

Twirling is so much harder than it looks. You have no idea.

"Okay, stop." Ginny forces a smile. She's trying to be nice to me, but her encouraging smile is starting to look a little strained around the edges. "I think we need to start with something easier."

I hold the baton still. It no longer seems like a wand, more like an instrument of self-torture. "Good. The easier, the better."

"Let's try a salute. It's super easy, but also important. Every baton routine begins with a salute to the judges." She takes the baton from my hands, flips it around, and gives it back to me. "You're holding it upside down again."

"Sorry." I grab it in the middle. So far, wrapping my fingers around the baton's silver stick is the only thing I've managed to master.

Ginny flashes me a grin of encouragement. "Okay, now flip your wrist."

I do as she says, and voilà—I don't bonk myself in the head. Instead, I manage to whack Ginny in the nose.

She lets out a yelp and covers her face with her hands.

"Oh my God, I'm so sorry. Are you okay?" I drop the baton like a hot potato, and it bounces a few times—head, toe, head, toe. My career as a twirler will never take off, but at least I learned something.

Ginny swishes past me, deftly moving around the baton without so much as stubbing her toe on it, and sinks onto the bed. "I can't look. Tell me—am I bleeding?"

"No." Thank *God*. "But I think I should get you some ice, as a precautionary measure. You probably don't want any more swelling."

"You think?" She groans, then flops backward so she's stretched out on the bed. "Today's a disaster. Yesterday was a disaster, and the day before was, too. What did I do to deserve this?"

Unknowingly steal my fiancé, maybe?

I shake my head as if I can rattle the unwelcome thought right out of my mind. Ginny did nothing wrong. Adam was an unfaithful jerk. I'm lucky I found out just how awful he was before I walked down the aisle and made the biggest mistake of my life. I dodged a bullet.

End of story.

"Nothing." My throat goes dry. "You've done nothing wrong. It's just a bad week. Everyone has those occasionally."

Ginny shoots me a wry glance.

"Maybe not *everyone.*" Has Ginny ever had a bad day in her life? Not that I can recall. This week excluded, obviously. "It will get better. I promise."

It can't get much worse. That's for sure.

"Sit tight. I'm going to get ice." I grab the plastic ice bucket from the bathroom counter. "I'll be right back."

Buttercup follows me to the door. I'm not sure if she thinks she's going for a walk, or if she just wants to stay glued to my side. I don't know what's going on with her, but suddenly she's my biggest fan. She's barely paid any attention to Ginny lately. The little bulldog even slept at the foot of *my* bed, not my sister's, which isn't helping Ginny's mood.

"Stay here," I whisper to the dog. I hold up my hand in the universal signal for stop. "Do you hear me? Stay."

Buttercup plops her little bottom onto the ground in a perfect sitting position. I'm astounded. She knows commands? When did that happen?

"You have some explaining to do, dog," I mutter. Then I slip out the door before she can follow me.

Halfway to the ice closet at the end of the hall, I realize I forgot to put on Ginny's Miss Texas sash before I left the room. Nor am I in perfect pageant form. My face is bare—

I'm not wearing a speck of makeup. I'm not even wearing shoes. I'm barefoot, wearing ripped, faded jeans, and one of my bookish T-shirts.

Curiouser and curiouser!

It's from *Alice's Adventures in Wonderland*, by Lewis Carroll, the actual author of the book. My students are always shocked and dismayed to learn it was written by a mathematician in the mid-nineteenth century and not Johnny Depp.

But I digress.

If anyone from the pageant spots me like this, I'm toast. So I duck my head and make a mad dash for the door marked *Ice* in hopes that no one will see me. I push the door open, dart inside, and then slam the door shut, leaning my forehead against the smooth wood.

My relief is short-lived.

As it turns out, I'm not alone in the tiny room. Behind me, a throat clears. A deep, masculine-sounding throat.

It can't be.

But it is.

My breath clogs in my throat, and I close my eyes and turn around. Maybe if I can't see him, he somehow won't be able to see me.

No such luck. When I open my eyes, he's still there. *Him.*

Gray Beckham is standing by the ice machine, watching me in all his brooding, Darcyesque glory.

I think I might faint. I wish I would, actually. Escaping

this awkward moment seems like a great idea, even if it involves temporary unconsciousness on my part.

But I don't faint. I just stand there like an idiot, staring into his dreamy blue eyes. My hands shake so violently that I nearly drop the ice bucket. I'm not sure whether I'm thrilled to see him, or whether I want to dash back down the hall and shut myself back inside the room with Ginny.

"You," I say breathlessly.

"You," he echoes. His tone is far less flattering.

I suddenly have no idea what to say. I waited in the stairwell for nearly an hour last night, hoping for a glimpse of him. I've taken Buttercup outside at least ten times since the ill-fated cheeseburger party. For the past sixteen hours, I've basically been stalking Gray Beckham and now that he's here, standing less than a foot away, I can't seem to form words.

"Excuse me." He moves to sidestep around me.

He's leaving. Of course he is. Why would he want to stay and flirt with me again after the way I've behaved?

"Wait." I leap in front of him, blocking his path.

He shifts the other direction, and so do I. As ridiculous a notion as it seems, it almost feels like we're dancing. If we were, it would be one of those intense love-hate dances. A tango, maybe? I'm not sure. Maybe his judge friend, the *Dancing with the Stars* alum, could shed some light on it.

"What are you doing?" Gray Beckham pins me with a glare, and my knees go weak.

He's so handsome. *Too* handsome. And despite the thunder in his gaze, I know that somewhere deep down, he likes me.

Or he used to, anyway.

"I'm apologizing." Something dangerous is unspooling inside me. I feel like my heart is about to fall out of my chest and land at his feet.

He arches a brow. "Apologizing?"

"Yes. I said some things yesterday that I wish I could take back. Terrible things." I take a deep breath and wait for some kind of sign that he's going to let me off the hook. But my hopes are dashed when his stony expression remains unchanged. "What I'm trying to say is that I'm sorry. I didn't realize why you were here."

He smirks and points to the judge pin on his lapel—the one I mocked earlier.

Of course he's wearing it. Unlike me, he's adhering to the pageant rules. He's also wearing another impeccable suit, looking like he just walked off the cover of the International Best-Dressed List issue of *Vanity Fair*. I remind myself that he went to Harvard. He's a tech genius. He's a *billionaire*.

I might have convinced myself a few days ago that he was an outsider, just like I am, but I was wrong. The only outsider here is me.

"I knew *why*, obviously. You're a judge. But I didn't know

who you were. I didn't know about your sister or the Miss Starlight pageant." Impossible, if I were a legitimate contestant. Which I'm not. But Gray Beckham isn't privy to that information.

He's still not saying anything, so I continue my constant stream of babble, digging an even bigger hole for myself.

"I know that doesn't make sense. I probably sound crazy. But I'm not. My situation is"—*fraudulent. Duplicitous. Pathetic*—"complicated."

I squirm while he continues glaring at me—except it's not quite a glare anymore. Some of the hostility has left his gaze, and now he's just looking at me as if I'm a puzzle he can't quite figure out.

"Complicated," he finally echoes. Then he takes in my shirt and his gaze moves slowly over the *Alice* quote. "'Curiouser and curiouser,' indeed."

I don't know how to respond. Even if I did, I'm not sure I could form words at this point. Now that I've gotten my apology off my chest, I'm acutely aware of how close we're standing to each other. He's inches away, and the tiny closet feels so small. So intimate.

I'm no longer holding the ice bucket between us as a barrier. My arms are hanging limply at my sides, and the plastic bucket dangles from my fingertips.

He tilts his head. "Why do I get the feeling you'll eventually end up leading me straight down the rabbit hole?"

If you only knew.

I should be relieved he's still standing here, willing to speak to me. And I am. But I'm also undeniably turned on. I know it's wrong. As much as I've managed to confess, he still has no idea who I am. Or that I'm a big, fat cheater.

But there's a delicious heat flowing through me all of a sudden. Our conversation has taken a beguiling little turn, and I like it. I like it far more than I should.

Why does he have to have a degree in English literature? *Why?* It makes him altogether too irresistible to a bibliophile like myself. Words from *Alice's Adventures in Wonderland* are spinning in my head and I have to bite my tongue to stop myself from rising up on tiptoe, pressing my lips to his ear, and whispering, "Drink me."

I clear my throat. But when I speak, my voice still comes out raw, with just a touch of ache. "I don't think you're a creep. Nor do I think you should move into Slytherin. Clearly you belong in Gryffindor."

He laughs, and the sound of it makes me want to weep with relief. "Gryffindor? That's high praise. Are you sure about that?"

"Absolutely. If anyone belongs in Slytherin, it's me." I'm the bad person in this scenario. I've told so many lies in the past few days that I'm starting to believe them.

He shakes his head. "I find that hard to believe, Hermione."

The reappearance of my nickname makes me glow, and when he says it, I happen to be looking straight at his mouth.

I'm not just looking, though. I'm also thinking—wondering about things I shouldn't, like what his lips would feel like against the hollow of my throat. Nice, probably. Warm. Soft. Perfect.

"Can I tell you a secret?" I hear myself ask.

My heart beats hard. Its rhythm pounds in my ears, and it sounds like a chant. *Tell him, tell him, tell him.*

"Anything," he says, and I swear he's looking at my mouth in the same delicious way I'm regarding his.

The ice bucket clatters to the ground, and neither of us react.

"I shouldn't be part of this pageant. I don't actually belong." As the words leave my mouth, I realize that I'm not just trying to confess. I'm also giving voice to my deepest secret—the terrible feeling I've been carrying around since Adam told me he'd fallen in love with my twin.

I don't belong *anywhere.*

I'm invisible.

Ginny is more beautiful than me. More confident. Just . . . *more.* And I'm not only hiding or pretending. I'm slipping away. I'm becoming less and less, and sometimes I think I might disappear altogether.

"Nonsense." He reaches to brush my hair from my face,

then takes my chin between his thumb and forefinger, forcing me to meet his gaze. "'We're all mad here.'"

It's another *Alice* quote, and this time, it's too much. I've opened myself up to him, just a crack, but it's enough to let the light in. *His* light. It feels like sunshine, flooding me with life and heat and something I haven't let myself feel in far too long.

Desire.

I want the feeling to last. I want to grab hold of this moment and make it mine. I want to kiss this man who somehow seems to see me, the *real* me, when no one else does.

So I do.

12

The kiss is even better than I imagined.

And yes, I've been imagining kissing Gray Beckham for quite some time. If I'm being honest, I've wanted to kiss him since the first night we met in the stairwell.

I just never thought I actually would.

I've no idea if he feels the same way. I want to believe we've been barreling toward this, that all our charming little encounters have been leading up to this moment and the attraction is really, truly mutual. But I'm afraid to let myself believe. If it's not true—if I've been dreaming about a mad love affair when he's simply been being polite—I will die. I can't stand any more humiliation in the name of attraction. I absolutely cannot. Dig a hole in the ground, shove me inside, and forget I ever existed because I'm done.

Excellent news, though. There's nothing polite about the way he kisses me back. Better yet, there's no hesitation.

No doubt. When I wrap my arms around his neck and press my lips to his, he groans. *Groans!*

That tantalizing sound is all the confirmation I need.

He's been thinking about kissing me too, it seems. The realization that I'm not alone in this—that he wants me as much as I want him—is enough to make me weak in the knees. I think I might faint for real this time. I sway a little, but before my legs give out, Gray presses me against the closed door, leaning into me and anchoring my hands above my head while he continues kissing me as if I'm the most desirable woman in the building. In the universe, maybe.

Oh my God.

This isn't polite at all. In fact, it's downright naughty. And I *love* it. I love how warm his mouth is—searing hot. I love the way I can feel his heartbeat crashing against mine when he leans closer. I even love the way he wads my nerdy, bookish T-shirt in his fist, clenching it tight before releasing it and sliding his hand up the side of my neck to bury his fingertips in my hair.

My body is aflame, head to toe.

Is this what kissing is supposed to feel like? Because it's not like any kiss I've ever experienced before. Heat is coursing through me, making me act in ways that are completely foreign to me. I'm biting at Gray's lower lip, whimpering against his mouth, begging and pleading for more—more of his witty words and soulful glances, more of his firm, muscular body.

More of *him*.

Somewhere amid the heady fog of desire, I'm fully aware of the wrongness of what's happening. He's a *pageant judge*. I try to tell myself it's okay because I'm not really a contestant.

But what I am is actually worse. I'm a phony. And a liar. There's no possible way that a man who runs a charity for terminally ill children will be okay with what I've done.

Nothing good can come of this.

I know I should stop. And I try. I really do, but my brain has turned to mush. If you asked me who J. K. Rowling is right now, I'd probably say she is the president of the United States. He's quite literally kissed me senseless.

I purr like a kitten. Then Gray's lips leave mine and just as I'm beginning to mourn their loss, his mouth drops to my neck. I can't take it anymore. The way he's pinned my arms above my head is undeniably hot—like, Heathcliff-stomping-around-the-windswept-moors-in-*Wuthering-Heights*-level hot—but I need to touch him.

"Please," I whisper, tugging free from his hand, still wringing my wrists like bracelets.

He lets them go, then rests his forehead against mine. Our gazes collide and for the first time, I notice the tiny gold flecks in his eyes as my hands find his chest. At last I'm touching him, letting my hands roam to his sides, sliding beneath his suit jacket and up the muscular expanse of his back.

A lump clogs in my throat. He feels so solid beneath my fingertips. So hard. So *real*. He kisses me again, but this time the kiss is tender—more reverent than I deserve.

My eyes begin to fill.

Then the door behind me bumps against my back, and I freeze.

We both do.

"Hello? Is someone in there?" The voice is feminine and familiar. It definitely belongs to one of the Miss American Treasure contestants, and she's obviously right on the other side of the door.

We've been caught. Our secret, forbidden tryst has lasted less than fifteen minutes.

"What do we do?" I mouth.

My heart is hammering so hard that I can feel it in my throat. What's going to happen now? Will Gray be fired? Will I have to wear a big scarlet *A* on the front of my gown during the evening-wear prelims?

Will Ginny tear me limb from limb for ruining her last shot at the crown?

Yes to that last one, obviously.

"Shhh," Gray whispers, raising a finger to his lips in a shushing motion.

I try to nod, but I can't. I'm paralyzed with fear.

The impatient beauty queen bangs on the door again. Who needs ice that badly? What's going on out there?

Slowly, carefully, Gray's hand moves toward the doorknob. I watch, wide-eyed, as he presses the pushbutton lock, trapping us inside.

I shoot him a questioning glance. What's his plan? Do we live here now in the ice closet? I could probably get on board with that.

But as it turns out, he's just buying time. He grabs his full ice bucket from the ledge of the icemaker, tucks it under his arm, and winks at me.

"Stay here until the coast is clear," he murmurs.

I blink.

And then he quietly unlocks the door, and before I can say a word, he slips out into the hallway, clicking the door closed behind him.

"Hello there," he says to the person on the other side. "Sorry, I think there's something wrong with the door. It's jammed."

"Oh, Mr. Beckham. Hi." The beauty queen's voice is now brimming with adoration. "I didn't realize you were in there."

"I was. But I'm not now. I'm out here in the hallway. With you," he says.

I stifle a giggle. He's almost as bad a liar as I am. Correction: as I used to be. Practice makes perfect and all that.

"Right. Well, would you mind stepping aside? I just need to get some ice." Her voice sounds closer.

What do I do now? Lock myself in?

"There's none left. I got the last of it," Gray says. "But here, you can have mine."

I take it back. He's actually rather good at thinking on his feet . . .

Among other things.

"Really? Are you sure?" The beauty queen is still lingering.

I am in *agony*. I've got to get out of here before someone sees me.

Just take the ice!

"Absolutely. I insist." I can hear a smile in Gray's voice. He's being chivalrous. And even though I know he's doing it to protect me—to protect *us*—an irrational stab of jealousy hits me in the chest.

What is wrong with me?

I wasn't always like this. I promise I wasn't.

But finding out your fiancé actually prefers your twin sister does something to you. Something ugly. No matter how many times you try to tell yourself that you're better off on your own or that you're an amazing person completely apart from your twin, the resentment lingers.

I'm not sure I fully grasped the extent of the damage Adam's words did to me until this week while I've been taking Ginny's place. I don't like it, but I don't know how to make it go away.

I wish I did. I wish that very, very much.

"All right then," the beauty queen says. She and Gray are still so close that I can hear the ice cubes shifting in the bucket as he hands it to her. "Thank you so much."

Finally.

I stay right where I am, with my back pressed against the door, as the voices in the hallway recede. I'm so anxious to get out of here that I could jump right out of my skin, but I force myself to wait.

After a torturous minute of silence goes by, I crack the door open and peer into the hall. It's blessedly empty.

I sprint back to my room on wobbly legs. My hands are shaking so much that I have to swipe the card key in the lock three times before I get the little green light. When I finally do, I swing the door open and dash inside.

Home free. We didn't get caught.

Everything's fine, I tell myself. Nothing to worry about at all. It's all a-okay.

But it's not. Not really. That kiss—and everything that followed—was a monumental mistake. And it can't happen again, no matter how very much I want it to.

He's a judge, and I'm a fake contestant impersonating her twin sister. The situation is too problematic for words.

Now that I'm back in my hotel room, I realize how

lucky we were that someone interrupted us and put a stop to our improper shenanigans. I don't even want to consider what would have happened if the knock on the door hadn't shaken some sense back into me.

Except, I sort of *do* want to consider it. A lot.

But I won't. Because recent hijinks aside, I am generally a good person. An honest one. I don't even dog-ear my books, much less engage in the kind of Sandra Bullock–rom-com subterfuge I'm embroiled in at the moment.

I take a deep breath and make a promise to myself. I'm going to do whatever needs to be done to get Ginny to the finals, and then I'm telling Gray the truth. The whole, ugly lot of it. In the meantime, no more sneaking around with him. No more clandestine meetings in the stairwell or the ice closet. *Definitely* no more kissing.

"Where on earth have you been?"

I jump at the sound of Ginny's voice.

She rounds the corner from the direction of the bathroom, jams her hands on her hips, and studies me through narrowed eyes. "Um, didn't you forget something?"

You mean, like how to tell the truth?

I bow my head, certain that she'll know what I've been up to if I look at her head-on. My gaze drops to the floor, and I notice that Buttercup is miraculously still sitting in the exact spot where I left her. She's peering up at me with her round, googly, Frenchie eyes, waiting to be praised.

I scoop the dog into my arms and cast a fleeting glance at Ginny over the top of her head. "Like what?"

I should probably know what she's talking about it, but for the life of me, I can't remember. My head is still back down the hall with Gray. And so, I fear, is my heart.

Ginny throws her hands up. "The *ice*."

Oh yeah.

The ice.

"Sit down. We need to talk," Ginny says, motioning for me to take a seat at the foot of her bed.

I've managed to convince her that when I got to the ice closest, the big, rumbling machine was empty. Then, because I'm such a great sister, I went to five other floors, but none of them had ice either. Somewhere in my epic quest for frozen water, I lost our ice bucket.

I feel a tad bit guilty that I've made myself out to sound like such a devoted twin in this complete and utter fabrication, but it's the only believable excuse I can come up with off the top of my head.

What am I supposed say?

Oops! I was so busy letting Judge Number Six kiss me silly that I forgot all about the fact that I hit you in the face with a baton.

So much nope.

"What's up?" I ask.

Truly, what could it possibly be? I can't take any more surprises. My nerves are more frayed than Mrs. Bennet's in *Pride and Prejudice*.

Ginny sighs and presses a plastic bag of ice against the rapidly forming bruise on the bridge of her nose. We ordered the ice from room service. Thankfully, they didn't rat me out.

"Come on, Charlotte. We both know what's going on here."

I swallow. "We do?"

Okay, maybe the room service people did tattle on me and tell her the hotel is, in fact, full of ice. It's practically an igloo. Or worse, maybe she's found out about Gray and me.

I feel sick. Buttercup seems to sense my panic and crawls into my lap.

What is up with this dog? Does she think Ginny and I have actually switched places?

"What's going on is that you can't twirl." Ginny drops her ice pack and gestures toward her head. "As evidenced by my face."

"In all fairness, I'm only responsible for your nose," I retort.

I'm *so* not in the mood for her criticism. Can't she see

how hard I've been trying? Does she have any inkling at all how miserable this whole charade makes me?

Of course she doesn't, and that's my fault.

I wonder what would happen if she knew the truth about why Adam and I broke up. Would she have still asked me to take her place?

Probably.

Maybe.

Or maybe not.

I'll never know, because it's too late. I'm swimming in sequins, and I can't back out. We're in the home stretch. In a matter of days, the prelims will be over and the top twenty will be announced. I've got a shot at this. Or . . . *she's* got a shot.

Except she's right. I can't twirl, and the talent prelims start in just a few hours.

I take a deep breath. "What are we going to do?"

"You're going to have to sing," she says.

"No." I shake my head. Hard. "No way."

My sister is fully aware that I can't carry a tune. Once, when we were in high school and Ginny was trying to rack up volunteer hours for yet another pageant and I needed service hours for my college applications, we went Christmas caroling together at a local nursing home. Midway through "O Holy Night," the activity director asked me to lip-synch, I kid you not.

Ginny was given a solo, because of course she was.

I did the rest of my service hours at the Dallas Food Bank.

"Look, it's not like any of these girls are Beyoncé or anything," Ginny says.

Is she sure about that? Has she seen Jordan Collins, Miss American Treasure 2013? Because she and Queen Bey look more like identical twins than Ginny and I do.

"A handful of the contestants have actual talent, but most everyone is faking it. Trust me. You can do this." Ginny smiles, but I can tell it's forced. She doesn't have any more confidence in my vocal abilities than I do.

She's desperate. If I don't show up and display some sort of talent, it's over. For both of us.

But I can't even bring myself to try karaoke at the school carnival. Two Halloweens ago, when the principal put me in charge of the karaoke booth, I traded places with the teacher who ran the cake walk. Because I knew the kids would try and goad me into singing something.

Also because cake.

"I can't." Gray will be there. Watching me. *Judging* me. I'd never get through the first verse of whatever show tune Ginny has in mind. It's always a show tune, isn't it? Either that, or opera. Which is *beyond* out of the question. "Let me rephrase. I *won't*."

I'm putting my foot down. I'd rather quit the pageant than sing.

"Then what do you propose?" she asks through gritted teeth.

Just as I'm about to revisit the idea of a dramatic reading, Buttercup lets out a timely snort. My gaze flits to the dog, and a crazy idea pops into my head.

So crazy that it just might work.

13

For the record, Ginny thinks I'm making a huge mistake. Shocker, I know.

She's so against the idea of incorporating a live animal into my performance that she caved on the dramatic reading front. She practically begged me to do a Shakespearean monologue, but I refused.

That's right—I finally stood up for myself. Although, I guess technically I stood up for Buttercup.

After learning she could sit and stay, I wondered what other tricks she might have in her repertoire. As it turned out, she knows quite a few. Don't get me wrong—she's no doggy Einstein or anything. But she knows how to sit, lie down, and shake.

After a few hours of practice, and a lot of treats, I've taught her how to give kisses on command. And I've also managed to get her to play dead, although that particular trick isn't too reliable. She only does it about half the time, but I'm still incorporating it into our routine. Worst-case scenario, she gets up and I crack a joke or something.

Right, because now you're a pageant queen, a stand-up comedian, and *a dog trainer.*

"I still think maybe you should do that thing from *Macbeth*," Ginny says as I slip a bedazzled Miss American Treasure tank top over Buttercup's head.

She and Ginny wear the same size shirt. Let that sink in for a minute.

"Nope." I shake my head. "Trust me. I've got this."

Ginny sighs. For a minute, I consider letting her in on exactly what I've got planned. But I can't. She'd never, ever go for it.

I, on the other hand, am brimming with confidence.

For once in my life.

"Can you get one of the other girls to record your performance? Even if it's just from the wings. I really want to see it." Ginny hands me her phone.

I tuck it into the bedazzled tote bag dangling from my elbow that holds treats for Buttercup and a few other things that my sister doesn't need to know about.

"I'll do my best." Like the swimsuit competition, the talent preliminaries are conducted for a private audience consisting solely of the six judges.

But I'm sure the contestants waiting in the wings will be

watching. If we go in alphabetical order again, I can probably get Torrie to tape it for me.

"Okay." I slip the Miss Texas sash over my head. "I think
we're ready."

"I'm so nervous I feel sick." Ginny flops down onto the
bed.

Welcome to my world.

"Wish us luck." I slip into the nude platform stilettos
and wobble toward the door. I lobbied hard for more prac-
tical attire, but Ginny wouldn't budge.

I tell myself that's fine. I can deal with the shoes. I've worn
them so much in the past few days that my feet are already
shredded to bits. What's a half-dozen more Band-Aids?

Besides, things could be worse. I could be headed downstairs to sing the aria from *Madama Butterfly*.

"Good luck." Ginny sits up to issue more last-minute
instructions. "Make sure you smile. And remember—you're
only allowed ninety seconds onstage, so don't try to do too
much. If you don't wrap things up quickly enough, the emcee will cut you off mid-performance. You'll definitely have
points deducted from your score."

I'm not worried about going over my allotted time. If
anything, I'm concerned about how to stretch six or eight
tricks into a full minute and a half. "Buttercup and I have
been practicing all afternoon. You've been timing us. We'll
be fine."

She nods. "Just don't forget the most important thing."

"What's that? Actually possessing talent?"

"No. The most important thing is eye contact! I've told you so a million times."

She has. I've just been trying not to dwell too much on it. I've managed to convince myself that I won't make a complete and total idiot of myself out there, but the thought of making eye contact with Gray Beckham is daunting, to say the least.

"Right," I mutter, fumbling with the doorknob.

"Don't forget," Ginny calls after me. "It's super important."

I shut the door behind me without making any promises in the eye-contact department.

"Come on, Buttercup," I whisper. "Let's do this."

When we arrive downstairs, the scene in the ballroom looks like an open call for *America's Got Talent*. Everywhere I turn, I see women wearing beaded gowns and wielding musical instruments. Ukuleles, flutes, clarinets, and violins. There's even an actual tuba. Most of the contestants who don't have an instrument tucked under their arms are either wearing dance costumes or going through the vocal scales. From where I'm standing, I can hear "Memory" from *Cats* coming at me from three different directions.

I take a deep breath and hug Buttercup a little tighter, trying to get my bearings. A ballerina twirls past me on pointe. I can see batons being tossed into the air, and I know without a shadow of a doubt that giving up the twirling was a good call.

Still, I can't help but feel a little out of my depth. Also, I'm the only person here who's holding an animal. I'm either about to make a complete fool of myself, or nail this competition. I get the sense there's no middle ground. Either way, Buttercup and I are sure to be memorable.

"Oh my gosh." Torrie's eyes widen when she spots me. "You've got a dog."

"I do." I can't tell if she's impressed or horrified. "This is Buttercup."

"She's precious. But I don't get it. Is she part of your talent? It says in the program that you're a twirler."

I nod. "There's been a slight change in plans."

Ginny called the pageant director earlier and requested a change. Thank goodness it was approved. She said she'd recently suffered a twirling mishap and wasn't sure she could bring herself to touch her baton again so soon. Which was all technically true, I suppose.

Miss Virginia walks past us and does a double take. "Oh. My. God. Is that a *dog*?"

Buttercup snorts. "Um . . ."

"It's part of her talent," Torrie says.

"She's adorable! Look at those eyes. Sooo cute." Miss

Virginia waves more people over with the bow from her violin. "Look, y'all! Ginny's talent is a dog."

Within seconds we're surrounded by a mob of fawning beauty queens, mostly girls from Torrie's cheeseburger party. They all *ooh* and *aah* over Buttercup. The little dog seems a little overwhelmed by the attention and starts shivering in my arms. My stomach plummets. The last thing I need is for her to get stage fright.

"What does she do?" Torrie says. "Does she ride a skateboard? I saw a bulldog do that once on television, and it was precious."

"No." I smile. "No skateboard."

Torrie sighs. "Oh. Does she ride a tricycle?"

I shake my head.

"A scooter?" Miss Virginia offers.

My smile grows tight. "No."

Miss Nevada goes wide-eyed. "OMG. Does she ride *another dog*?"

My smile disappears altogether. "No. I thought you were a veterinarian. Are dogs riding dogs even a thing?"

She shrugs. "You'd be surprised."

"I don't get it." Miss Virginia shoots Buttercup a dubious look. "If she doesn't ride anything, what does she do? What do *you* do?"

"I give her commands and she does tricks. You know, basic dog things like sit and speak." I look down at Buttercup and she swivels her big eyes toward me. Even she's starting to look doubtful about this whole thing.

"Oh," Torrie says. A few of the other contestants exchange glances. "I'm sure it's super cute."

"It is," I say defensively. "It's more than cute. We've got a theme and everything. It's actually kind of brilliant."

I'm not sure who I'm trying to convince, myself or the crowd of bedazzled naysayers. All I know is that if I allow myself to think for even a second that I'm about to crash and burn, I'll never get up on that stage.

It was different when the only thing at stake was Ginny winning the crown. I mean, I wanted her to win, of course. Following in our mom's footsteps means the world to her. That's the entire reason why I agreed to all of this to begin with.

But somewhere along the way, things have shifted. I want to do well. Does that sound crazy? Never mind. I know it does. It's completely ridiculous. I have a life back at home. A real life where no one expects me to look good in a bikini, walk in high heels, or possess any sort of talent.

Maybe that's the problem, though. Maybe we all need a little push now and then. Maybe there's some truth to what everyone says about venturing out of your comfort zone. Blah blah blah.

That has to be it. Because my sudden interest in making

the top twenty—on my own terms—can't have anything to do with Gray Beckham. All of that's over. Period.

Except when I see him enter the room and take a seat at the judges' table, my heart leaps to my throat. He's wearing the same suit he had on earlier in the ice closet. And he looks spectacular, all piercing blue eyes and exquisite bone structure. Even Buttercup notices. I swear she sighs in my arms.

Just as I'm about to look away, my gaze snags. There's something off about Gray's appearance. Something not quite as perfect as the rest of him. My face goes hot when I finally put my finger on it. His tie is a little mussed. It looks like it's been smoothed down flat after someone tried to wring it out like a dishrag.

And that someone is me.

I cough. Somewhere in the back of my head, I have a vague recollection of grabbing that pale blue necktie and holding on tight, anchoring myself to Gray as he kissed me.

Why is he still wearing it? He's got to have other ties.

I tell myself that it doesn't mean anything. He's a man. He's in tech. He's a successful millionaire. *Billion*aire. Whatever. He's probably so type A that he's got a tie for each day of the week, and he doesn't want to throw a wrench in things by switching midday. The silk Hermès that so perfectly accentuates the color of his eyes is just his Thursday tie.

But then, for the briefest of moments, our eyes meet across the crowded room. Ever so subtly, he straightens his

Windsor knot, then moves his fingertips down the length of his tie in a smoothing motion. Then he looks away.

It's a secret message. I know it is. I'm just not altogether sure what it means, because I'm so totally in over my head. Last week I was shelving picture books and now I've got more secret lives than I can keep up with. I've somehow become the beauty pageant version of Jason Bourne.

"Still think he's creepy?" Torrie says, following my gaze.

Super. I just got caught staring at Gray Beckham.

I clear my throat and turn my back toward him since I obviously can't be trusted to ignore his presence in my line of sight. "No, I don't. The Miss Starlight thing is amazing. *He's* amazing."

Torrie's head tilts. "Is he, now?"

My chest goes tight. I was wrong about not having any talent. When it comes to sticking my foot in my mouth, I've got oodles. "I mean, you know, he's an amazing philanthropist."

"Oh, sure." She aims her gaze over my shoulder. "Plus he's hot. Look at him."

I shake my head. "No, thank you. I don't want to look at him."

Buttercup plants her head on my shoulder. Without even checking, I know she's also staring at Gray.

Torrie gives me a look that translates roughly into *Even the dog wants to look at him. What's wrong with you?*

I swallow. What *is* wrong with me? "I've already looked at him, and I think I've seen enough. You know what I mean."

Buttercup snorts. If I wasn't relying so heavily on her to get me through the talent competition, I'd tell her she was a bad dog. A *very* bad dog.

"Actually, I don't know what you mean," Torrie says.

Neither do I. I'm just saying things—things that make no sense whatsoever—and I can't seem to stop. Gray's presence is unnerving me. As is his rumpled tie and his lush mouth and as Torrie puts it, his hotness.

I'm also convinced that she can sense what I've done—that it's somehow written all over my face. Is there a facial expression that says *I've been making out with the pageant judge in the ice closet?* Because if there is, I'm surely rocking it right now.

Fortunately, before I can spew any more nonsense, the pageant production assistant in the sparkly Miss American Treasure jacket is back, wielding her ubiquitous clipboard. "Ladies, find your places backstage please. We're starting in ten."

I'm grateful for the respite from the awkward conversation, even if it means Buttercup and I are within minutes of our performance. Torrie drops the subject of Gray immediately and begins going over her contemporary dance number in her head, counting to herself as we head backstage.

We line up in the wings, again in alphabetical order according to state. The production assistant runs back and forth, checking things off on her clipboard. Unlike the swimsuit competition the day before, there's no happy chatter backstage. Every contestant is in her own little world, mentally rehearsing for her performance.

Good idea.

I plop Buttercup down on the floor, and she gazes up at me, wide-eyed. I give her the hand signal for sit—the one we've been practicing for hours.

She doesn't budge.

A flare of panic seizes me.

I try the command again. Still, nothing.

What's happening? Is it possible we've overrehearsed? I try the hand signal three more times and finally, Buttercup sits. I choose to believe she was suffering a little stage fright and she's finally had a breakthrough. The more obvious explanation is that she simply got tired of standing, but I can't allow my mind to go there.

I'm afraid to attempt anything else. We're running out of time anyway. Four contestants ran through their numbers in the span of time it took for Buttercup to sit. Awesome.

I crouch down beside the dog and remove her Miss American Treasure tank top. Ginny would have my head if she could see me. I've officially veered from the preapproved plan and implemented my own. I've gone rogue. But hey, I'm Jason Bourne. Everything will be fine.

God, I hope it will.

I rummage through my tote bag for the other things I need. After I've put Buttercup in her new costume and tucked my prop under my arm, I consider Ginny's phone. Should I ask someone to record our routine or not?

The announcer's voice booms over the loudspeaker. "Please welcome Miss Tennessee to the stage."

Things are happening at warp speed. It's already Torrie's turn. I give her a quick hug for good luck and shove Ginny's phone back into my bag.

Torrie's dance is impressive. Then again, I'm impressed by all the performances, since the only thing I can manage to dredge up is a silly routine with a dog. She stumbles out of one of her turns, and for a split second her smile falters. But it's back in an instant, and she maintains her eye contact with the judges until her final step. The way she's staring at them is almost aggressive, as if she's daring them to give her a bad score.

My stomach flips. There's no way I can maintain that kind of brash confidence.

"Thank you, Miss Tennessee. And now let's have a round of applause for Miss Texas!"

It's time.

I cast a final glance at Buttercup and shoot her an encouraging smile, then we walk to the center of the stage. Buttercup bobs happily at the end of her leash while I concentrate on not face-planting in my stilettos.

Once we're in position, I glance up to find the judging panel watching us with blatant curiosity in their eyes. I paste on a beauty queen grin.

Don't look at him. Don't look at Gray.

I can't help it. I look.

His expression is guarded. When our eyes meet, the corner of his mouth twitches, like he's trying not to smile.

Instantly, I start to sweat.

How am I going to get through this?

I stand, paralyzed, for a full second. I can practically hear the clock ticking in my head. Eighty-nine . . . eighty-eight . . .

I clear my throat. "I'm Miss Texas, and this is my assistant, Fang."

A few of the judges snicker. Gray doesn't, but he smiles so broadly it lights up the room . . . along with my heart.

"Actually, she's a rescue dog and her name is Buttercup, but for our act today, she's playing the part of Fang, a character in the beloved book series Harry Potter." I gesture toward the tiny black robe she's wearing. "Hence the wizard attire."

I can't believe it's only been a matter of days since I bought the robe at Harry Potter World. It seems like a lifetime ago. I originally purchased it for the big stuffed owl that sits on a shelf in the library at school, but desperate times call for desperate measures. And this, my friends, is desperation at its finest.

"Since Fang is a wizard, when it comes to training, I find that a touch of magic works wonders." I reach inside the pocket of my peplum jacket and pull out my plastic theme park wand.

The judges laugh out loud.

This is either going brilliantly, or I'm making an idiot out of myself.

In for a penny, in for a pound.

I aim the plastic wand at Buttercup and channel Hermione as best I can. "Let's see if Fang responds to a summoning spell, shall we?"

I keep my left hand low and angle my body so the judges can't see the hand signal I'm giving the dog. *Come.*

With my other hand, I give the wand a little swirl in the air while I call out, "Accio!"

Buttercup trots toward me, and I hear a collective gasp of approval. I'm not sure where it's coming from—either the contestants waiting in the wings or the judges.

Relief floods my veins. *It's working.*

I turn my back on Buttercup and take a few steps. She trots after me, like she's being doing for the past couple of days.

I turn and point the wand at her again. "Impedimenta."

She plops into a sit position.

With an arched brow, I tell the judges, "Just a little immobilization spell. It won't last long."

We go through a few more magic tricks in rapid succession. Buttercup lies down when I use the Stupefy spell and then rolls over when I call out Riddikulus.

Once the little dog is standing again, I say in a loud mock whisper, "I don't dabble much in the Dark Arts, but let's see if I've got what it takes to pull off a killing spell."

I wave the wand at Buttercup and using the hand that's hidden from the judges, I make a gun gesture with my thumb and pointer finger. "Avada Kedavra!"

Buttercup falls onto her side, playing dead.

The judges are collapsing into heaps of laughter now. All of them, including Gray. Because, yes, I look again. I can't help myself. And as embarrassing as it is to admit, the fact that he's impressed by my silly little act makes me giddy. Not because this is a contest and he's a judge, but because I care about his opinion. I care about *him*.

And in that instant, I know the kiss wasn't just a fluke or a one-time thing. It meant something . . . to me at least. And even though I vowed it was a mistake, if I had the chance to take it back, I wouldn't. In fact, I want to kiss him again.

Soon.

Right now, actually.

I want to toss my wand aside, cross the stage, and kiss him right here in front of everyone.

I don't, obviously. But the image is swirling in my head, taunting me while the ninety-second clock winds down.

That's when I realize I'm in trouble. So very much of it. I feel as though I've downed a gallon of Amortentia. Which, in case you're wondering, is the most powerful love potion in the world of Harry Potter.

I grip my wand so tightly that it's in danger of snapping in two. Buttercup rearranges her compact little body so that she's resting in a sphinxlike position, awaiting her next command.

We've only got time for one more trick, so I choose my favorite. This one doesn't even need a wand. Only a word.

Specifically, a name.

"Voldemort!" I say, invoking the name of Harry Potter's archenemy, the most dangerous wizard of all time. The Dark Lord. He-Who-Must-Not-Be-Named.

Buttercup responds as any smart dog would. She covers her face with her paws and lets out a whine.

The round of applause this elicits is so loud that I barely hear it when the head judge calls out, "Time."

And for a wild, wonderful moment, I believe in magic. I believe in the crown. I might even believe in myself.

14

Buttercup and I win the talent competition.

I hardly believe it. I was only trying to get through those ninety seconds and survive with enough points to keep Ginny in the top twenty. But when the emcee announces the winner of the talent prelims, it's my name that she calls.

Well, technically she calls Ginny's name.

But in this instance, Ginny's name is good enough. Because what I just did onstage with Buttercup wasn't my sister's talent routine. It was mine. For the first time in days, I performed as myself.

And I won!

I scoop Buttercup into my arms and return to the stage to accept our plaque, along with a huge bouquet of red roses. The bouquet is so lush that I can't hold on to it and Buttercup at the same time. I place her back down on the ground and she prances in place, seemingly aware that she's every bit as much a winner as I am in this scenario.

"Good girl," I tell her. "Very good girl."

Her big, batlike ears swivel to and fro.

All the hoopla feels nice. I can't deny it. I also can't deny that my sense of accomplishment would be greater if Gray Beckham weren't on the judging panel.

I tell myself that he's not the type of person who would give me a better score than I deserve. After all, between the two of us, I'm the dishonest one. Still, the memory of our recent, ahem, *encounter* looms.

I can't help feeling like I've cheated, and I don't just mean the whole pageant.

But as the emcee beams at me, she clears her throat and makes another announcement. "I'm happy to tell you, Miss Texas, that your performance received a near-perfect score. You received a ten from all but one of our judges."

I blink. "What?"

She means a ten from *one* judge, right? Not all but one of them. Gray obviously has a healthy appreciation for the literary works of J. K. Rowling, but I'm dubious about the rest of the judges. I can't exactly picture that guy from *The Bachelorette* with his head buried in a book.

There I go, jumping to conclusions again. Clearly I'm wrong, because the emcee meant what she said.

"You got five tens and one nine," she says.

My mind reels.

"Thank you." I sniff. My eyes fill. I did this. *I* did. I

would have won the talent prelim, even if Gray hadn't been on the panel. "Thank you so much."

I press the plaque to my heart with one hand and clutch the bouquet in my other. The roses are deep crimson, just like the ones resting in my mother's arms in the photograph on Ginny's nightstand.

I close my eyes, fighting the tears that are threatening to spill down my face. When I open them, I see the current Miss American Treasure coming toward me, carrying something sparkly.

It's a tiara.

The crown is much smaller than the one my mother wore, but the design is exactly the same.

My face crumples as she secures it to my head full of hair extensions and styling products. Tears stream down my cheeks. I have officially become a cliché. I'm one of those GIFs of sobbing pageant girls that make the rounds on social media every year when the Miss America pageant is televised. It's ridiculous.

But I can't help it. Other than playing dress-up with my mother's crown as a kid, this is the first time a tiara has ever come in contact with my head. Ginny's bedroom at Dad and Susan's house is stacked with them. It's practically a tiara warehouse. She's got homecoming queen tiaras and crowns from so many pageants that I'd never be able to name them all if I tried.

I was never envious of all my twin's beauty queen hardware. Honestly. At least not that I realized. But the crown feels so right on my head, and knowing that it looks just like my mother's did makes me never want to take it off.

Warmth blossoms in my chest. I take a deep breath—the deepest one I've taken in years. Something has shaken loose inside me. It seems that Ginny isn't the only one who's been walking around with a beauty queen–shaped hole in her heart.

I have too.

And this moment feels like a balm. I cling to it, holding on tight. And I try with all my might to remember that whatever happens when all of this is over will be worth it.

Because right here, right now, I'm where I belong.

In the excitement that follows, I lose track of Gray. He slips away at some point while I pose for pictures and am hugged and congratulated by all forty-nine of my fellow contestants.

I'm embraced so many times that my roses are starting to wilt. When I finally head back to the hotel room, I leave a trail of petals in my wake, like a flower girl at a wedding.

My head is buzzing. I can't wait to tell Ginny what just happened. But once I'm standing at our door with my card key poised just over the lock, I hesitate.

Seeing me in a tiara is going to sting. I know it will. I'm tempted to pry the thing off my head, even though Miss American Treasure anchored it in place with so many bobby pins that I'm not sure I'll ever be able to remove it.

I look down at Buttercup. "What do you think?"

Her response is nothing but a series of long, slow-motion blinks. The poor thing is exhausted. Cramming a month's worth of dog training into a single day will do that to a dog, apparently.

Message received. We can't keep hiding in the hallway. And it's not as if I can keep the tiara a secret from Ginny forever. Sooner or later, she'd sniff it out. Probably sooner. She has a nose for crowned jewels.

I slide my key into the lock, take a deep breath, and open the door. Then I pause, thoroughly confused by the sight of Ginny on the other side.

"Here you are," she says. "I thought I heard someone out there."

She's walking toward me with a strained smile plastered to her face. Her eyes are wild. Manic, almost. But her frenzied expression and unnaturally high-pitched voice aren't the only things that give me pause. What catches me most off guard are her clothes.

She's wearing my Hogwarts T-shirt. It hangs loosely on her, reaching halfway to her knees—a good two or three sizes larger than any shirt she would willingly put on. And are those my favorite sweatpants she's got on? The ones she almost didn't let me wear to the cheeseburger party?

Yes. Yes, they are.

"Um . . ." My gaze fixes with hers, and it's then that I notice her messy bun and lack of makeup. She looks like me, from head to toe, only her face is still swollen. So, more accurately, she looks like I would on an exceptionally bad day.

I glare at her.

Is this some kind of joke? She's mocking my usual appearance. But why?

"Come on in, silly." She grabs my hand, squeezing it hard when I try to pull away. "Look who's here."

I stumble into the room behind her, tripping over my high heels. Buttercup trails after me. Then two familiar faces come into view and I freeze. My beautiful bouquet of roses falls to the ground.

"Dad. Susan." I swallow. Hard. My heart is beating so hard that I might be on the verge of a panic attack. I probably am, because if ever there was a time to panic, it's now.

What on earth are our dad and stepmother doing here? They weren't scheduled to arrive until the start of the finals two days from now.

"That's right. They wanted to come early and surprise us, since we're both here together," Ginny says. "Aren't you surprised? I know I am."

Understatement. I'm beyond surprised. I'm aghast.

I'm so stunned to see them standing in our room that I'm rooted to the spot.

My twin moves closer to me and gives me a subtle jab in the ribs.

I jump, then propel myself toward our parents for a hug, since that's what Ginny would normally do. It's also what *I* would normally do if I weren't suddenly longing for a paper bag to breathe into. "Sorry, it's great to see you both. I just wasn't expecting you so soon."

My throat closes as I throw my arms around my dad. He'll never be fooled by this charade. He's *our father*. No amount of makeup and sparkle will trick him into believing I'm anyone but who I am.

But behind him, I spot Ginny again, dressed in her Charlotte attire. I'm not altogether sure what transpired while I've been competing, but clearly my sister had enough of a heads-up to transform herself into me. Granted, it was surely a much less time-consuming endeavor than what I went through to assume her identity.

Still.

As convincing as her dressed-down Charlotte costume may be, how has she managed to fool them for even a few minutes?

"Hi, honey," my dad says.

I don't trust myself to speak, so I just nod and shoot a panicked glance over his shoulder toward Ginny.

Susan wraps me in her arms the minute my dad releases me. She's been our stepmother for more than two decades, so she's not much more likely than our father is to fall for our switcheroo. She isn't my real mother, but she's the next best thing. She sat beside my dad in the stands and cheered for me when I graduated from both high school and college. She covered all the kitchen shelves in my first real apartment with scented contact paper. She took me shopping for my wedding gown. Two months later, she held me as I cried when I told her and Dad that the wedding had been called off.

So the odds that she won't recognize me are slim at best.

But when she pulls back from our embrace and plants her hands on my shoulders to take a good look at me, Susan doesn't flinch.

"Oh, Ginny. You look *beautiful*, sweetheart. Look at her, Ed. Isn't she just gorgeous?" Her gaze flits to my dad, who nods in his quiet dadlike way, and then back toward me. "And look at that tiara! What a sparkler. You've won something already!"

She bustles toward the bed and gives the space at the foot of it a little pat. "Sit down and tell us all about it."

Obediently, I follow her and sit down on the bed. Before I say anything to confirm the fact that I'm supposed to be Ginny, I search my sister's gaze.

Now is the time to come clean and tell our parents what

we've done. They're sure to be disappointed. Actually, that's probably an understatement. They're going to be pissed.

We weren't raised to be liars, especially when it comes to the whole twin thing. I have a very clear memory of being grounded for writing Ginny's English lit final paper when we were seniors in high school. And isn't what we're doing now essentially the exact same thing?

It is. I know it is. So does Ginny, although from the looks of things she has no qualms about keeping the charade going.

"Wow." Ginny crosses her arms and stares at my crown. In her rush to usher me inside and get me up to speed with the most recent development in our deception, she'd clearly overlooked it. "That is definitely a tiara."

Her gaze darts to the photo on her nightstand—the one of our mother. Ginny's chin wobbles, then she looks back at me.

"Actually . . . ," I begin.

Actually, I'm not Ginny. I'm Charlotte.

I'm doing it.

I'm ending this farce once and for all. We can't lie to our parents. So far, I haven't actually claimed to be Ginny in their presence. It's not too late.

But the words stick in my throat, because even though I haven't dragged Dad and Susan into our pageant hoax yet, Ginny obviously has. How long have our parents been here?

Minutes?

Hours?

She gives me an almost imperceptible shake of her head. The deed is done. They think she's me.

"Actually . . . ," I say again, stalling for time. I can't believe I'm going through with this. Switching places in the pageant is one thing. Doing so in front of our parents is another matter entirely. Lindsay Lohan was twelve years old when she played identical twins who switched places in *The Parent Trap*. We're *adults*, for crying out loud. "Yes, it's a tiara. I won the talent competition this afternoon."

"That's fantastic," Susan says, clapping her hands.

Dad beams. He hasn't looked at me with this much pride since I showed him the magna cum laude insignia on my college degree. *Seriously?*

"Wonderful, Ginny. Just wonderful," he says.

I nod and smile. *Yes, it's wonderful. And yes, I'm Ginny.*

It's official. I'm the world's worst daughter. I glance at my sister. Fine, it's a tie. We'll share the title, even though it's a far cry from the crown we've been chasing for the past few days.

"You're kidding, right?" Ginny's gaze narrows. "You *won*? As in, you had the highest score out of all fifty contestants?"

"That's generally what winning means," I say tightly.

Dad and Susan don't appear to notice any tension between the two of us, which should be a relief. But honestly, it's kind of a blow. The real Charlotte—as in *me*—is usually far more supportive of Ginny. At least I like to think she is.

But when I try to remember the last time the sight of my sister wearing a tiara elicited any sort of praise from my lips, I come up empty and an uncomfortable shame settles over me.

I didn't even come to Orlando to support her, did I? I'd planned on attending the finals, just like Dad and Susan. But the main reason I showed up was because I wanted a vacation.

Some holiday.

Nothing has gone as planned. Not one thing. Although I have to admit that this week has had its fair share of . . . *moments*.

As if on cue, my gaze flits to our new ice bucket.

"I guess all those twirling lessons paid off," Susan says.

"She didn't twirl," Ginny says flatly.

"Really? Why not? You worked so hard." Susan waits for an answer, and the room falls silent.

Oh, right. She's talking to me. She thinks I'm the one who's spent months practicing all that complicated head, toe, head, toe stuff. "I thought it might be nice to try something different. You know, more creative."

My word choice is less than ideal.

Ginny takes immediate offense. "Really? I thought you changed plans because you kept dropping your baton earlier."

"Charlotte." Dad's voice carries a hint of reprimand.

Ginny shrugs. "It's true. Ask her."

I sigh. Clearly we're *not* adults. We're being petty and childish, which is absurd. After all, we're in this together.

"Charlotte's right," I say. "I'm pretty terrible at twirling. Thank goodness Buttercup was here to save the day."

"You're kidding." My dad looks at Buttercup—fast asleep, snoring and grunting on my pillow—and laughs. "Forgive me, but I just can't picture that dog doing much of anything."

"She's a good dog," Ginny counters. "A *brilliant* dog, in fact."

Dad lifts a brow. "That's high praise coming from someone who just met her a few days ago. When did you become such an animal lover?"

The question is directed at my sister, but I intervene, since technically we're talking about me.

"Charlotte likes animals," I say. I don't *dis*like them, anyway.

"Since when?" Dad asks, sounding genuinely curious.

Ginny opens her mouth to respond, but again, I answer for her. "Since always. She just doesn't dress them up in sweaters and bunny ears and plaster them all over her Instagram page." I clear my throat. "You know, like I do."

Ginny nods. "It's super cute when you do that, though. Don't you think so, Dad?"

Our father glances back and forth between the two of us.

My stomach drops. *Oh God. He knows.*

I do my best to get the conversation back on track by launching into a detailed description of my talent routine. There's another shaky moment when Susan points out that Charlotte is the big Harry Potter fan in the family, not Ginny. But when I give Charlotte credit for coming up with the theme for the routine, she seems convinced.

Susan smiles at Ginny. "It's nice that you're helping your sister with the pageant, Charlotte."

If she only knew.

"I've been a big help. Huge," Ginny says. "But it means a lot to Ginny. I know it does, even if she forgets to say it sometimes."

It's the most sincere expression of appreciation I've gotten all week, and I can't help but get a little misty-eyed. I blink furiously before Dad or Susan grow suspicious again.

Keeping them in the dark is going to be impossible. We are *terrible* at this. I'm too much like myself for them to keep believing I'm Ginny. And Ginny is just too much, period.

Why haven't they figured it out yet? Especially Dad. I always thought I was his favorite. When I was a little girl and I'd spend hours tucked into the corner of his office with a book, he sometimes called me his mini me. How is it possible that he no longer knows who I am?

Is this what it was like with Adam? Did he see me at all, or did he simply prefer my twin? I'm not sure which option is less excruciating.

There's a knock at the door, and I'm grateful for the distraction. I know I should be glad that our ruse has gone undiscovered, but I can't help but feel a little unsettled. I'm not hiding anymore. I'm right here. And my own father doesn't even see me.

"Who could that be?" Ginny tenses, poised to run and hide in case the person responsible for the knock is somehow related to the Miss American Treasure pageant.

I almost hope it's the pageant director herself, just because I'd love to hear my sister explain to our parents why she needs to cower behind the shower curtain.

"I have no idea. Let me check." I push myself off the bed and head for the door. Buttercup rouses from her sleep and trots after me.

Ginny's not sticking around. "I have to go to the bathroom."

She dashes out of sight while Dad and Susan linger, oblivious to the drama unfolding around them.

Why does it feel like things are getting crazier by the minute around here?

Probably because they are.

I open the door a crack. To my extreme delight, the person standing on our threshold doesn't have a thing to do with the pageant. It's a room service waiter, and he's holding a fancy looking bottle of champagne. Veuve Clicquot, with a sleek orange label.

"Ginny Gorman?" he says.

"Um . . ." Who am I again? I swear I'm beginning to lose track. "Yes, that's me."

"This is for you." He hands me the bottle, along with a small white envelope. "Special delivery."

"Oh, wow. Thank you." At this particular moment in time, alcohol seems like either a fantastic idea or a really terrible one. Either way, I definitely plan on indulging. I'll take my chances.

"How many glasses do you require?"

I hold up four fingers with my free hand. "Four, please."

"Let me get that for you, sweetheart." My dad takes the bottle and hands me a few dollars to tip the waiter.

I trade the bills for four slender champagne flutes. Buttercup watches the transaction with rapt interest.

"Thank you, again," I say.

"My pleasure. Enjoy." The waiter glances at my tiara, smiles, and then disappears down the hall.

I shut the door, then swing around to face my parents. "Wow, champagne. Thanks so much, y'all."

Dad and Susan exchange a glance.

"It's not from us," Susan says.

"Oh." I shrug. "It must be a gift from the pageant for winning the talent competition."

Ginny emerges from the bathroom, slinking among us like a cat burglar. She should really work on her subtlety since she's so keen on living a double life.

"It was room service," I say, just as Dad pops the cork.

Ginny gives a little start at the noise.

She has *got* to calm down. I really doubt the waiter was an undercover spy for Miss American Treasure. He didn't even see her, for goodness' sake.

I shove a glass in her hand. "Here."

"Charlotte?" Susan says.

Ginny and I turn our heads in unison.

Oops.

"Should you be drinking while you're still on medication for your allergic reaction?" Susan pulls a face.

"I'll just have a tiny sip," Ginny says, while I make a big show of helping Dad as if I didn't accidentally think Susan was actually talking to me.

"When did you order this?" Ginny peers into her glass.

"I didn't. I think it's from the pageant." My dad hands me a glass and I take a sip. The champagne is ice-cold, and the fizzy bubbles dance on my tongue. Mmm. "Oh, I almost forgot. There's a card."

I look around for the small white envelope. I can't remember what I did with it. It's not on the dresser or any of the other cluttered surfaces in our cramped room.

Just when I think it's permanently buried beneath a pile

of glitter somewhere, I spot Buttercup in the corner, gnawing gleefully on something. Upon closer inspection, I see that it's my card.

"Gee, thanks." I pry it from her jaws.

It's a soggy mess, but still in one piece. With any luck, I'll be able to read what it says.

I slide the card from the envelope, and my heart swells. It's definitely readable, and I love what it says.

Well done, Hermione. Congratulations.

He didn't sign the card, but he didn't have to. I know the champagne was a gift from Gray. I'm suddenly glad I didn't cave and confess all to Dad and Susan. I'm not ready for this crazy ride to end.

Not yet.

Just one more day.

The swelling in Ginny's face has gone down nearly 75 percent, but now she's got a purple bruise across the bridge of her nose where I hit her with the baton. I want her to get better. Of course I do. But I'm not ready to switch back. It's too soon.

Just one more day.

It's running through my head like a mantra. I refuse to ask myself the obvious follow-up question. *And then what?*

"Well?" Ginny eyes the square of paper in my hand.

I wad the note into a ball in my fist, but I don't toss it into the trash. I save it, holding on tight to Gray's words. "It's from the pageant, just like I thought."

"That was nice of them." Ginny smiles and clinks her glass against mine. "And you deserve it. Congratulations, sis. Tomorrow is the evening-gown competition—the last stop before the finals. You know what that means."

A lump forms in my throat, and I can't bring myself to answer my twin because I do. I know exactly what it means.

Just one more day.

15

The early arrival of our parents changes everything.

At least they've got their own room. Thank God. But naturally, they want to have breakfast the next morning with us at the hotel's posh restaurant overlooking the infinity pool. Which would be lovely, if only it were in the realm of possibility.

Ginny and I can't be seen together. Trading places is risky enough when no one realizes there are two of us. If either Ginny or I get outed as an identical twin, our chances of getting caught would skyrocket. Also, Ginny being Ginny, she refuses to leave the room until her face is completely back to normal.

So I'm the lucky one who gets to explain to Dad and Susan why we only need a table for three at breakfast instead of four. Awesome. I hope and pray they're serving mimosas. It's the only thing keeping me going at this point.

When I get to the restaurant, my father and stepmom

are already seated, because being early for everything is apparently their new hobby. They could have taken up golf or joined a book club, but no. This is what they went with instead.

It's not that I don't love spending time with them. I do. I love it a lot. I just prefer hanging out with my family when I'm not cheating in a national beauty pageant by pretending to be my sister.

"Hi." I sit down and flash them a full-wattage, Ginny-esque smile. Our table is at the edge of the resort's cabana, shaded by a large patio umbrella and swaying palm trees. "It's so gorgeous out here. Gin . . . Charlotte and I have been eating mostly room service. We haven't had much of a chance to see the rest of this place."

"Good morning, honey." Dad smiles, then looks past me as if my twin is going to materialize out of thin air. "Where's your sister?"

"She's not up to coming down for breakfast. I think she still feels a little self-conscious about her allergy situation." I wave a hand at my face by way of explanation.

My father's brow furrows. "That doesn't sound like Charlotte."

"What do you mean?" I know I shouldn't ask, and the prickle at the back of my neck tells me I probably won't like the answer, but he and Susan are looking at me, waiting for me to say something.

He shrugs. "You know. Charlotte doesn't normally care much about her appearance."

Oh. We're going there.

I suppress the urge to ask him to elaborate. My dad thinks I don't care how I look? That's hurtful.

I *care*. I just care a normal amount instead of a beauty pageant amount. Granted, I usually don't wear makeup. And as Ginny so lovingly pointed out, my go-to hairstyle is a ponytail. But I *do* brush it before I put it up. I'm not a *total* mess, am I?

Susan chimes in, agreeing with him. "Exactly. Looks aren't really high on her priority list."

Et tu, Susan?

"She probably just wants to hole up in the room with her head in a book," Susan adds.

Super. So the whole family thinks I ordinarily look like a train wreck and that I'm a loner. I'm really not. Deep down, I know all my efforts to downplay my appearance and rail against the pageant scene have more to do with missing my mom than anything else. The makeup, tiaras, and fancy clothes remind me of her, and sometimes it's just easier to not have to see it all so I can forget a little bit.

A server swishes past our table and I silently beg for that mimosa I've been dreaming about. A pitcher of them would be nice.

"Well, this *is* Charlotte's vacation," I say in defense of myself.

If you ever want to hear what your family truly thinks of you—and trust me, you don't—have breakfast with them disguised as your sibling. It's an eye-opener.

I pick up my menu, and my stomach growls. Once again, I'm starving. Everything listed on the smooth ivory pages sounds delicious. I'm trying to decide between Belgian waffles or an omelet stuffed with everything when my dad clears his throat.

He leans closer and lowers his voice. "Speaking of Charlotte, do you know if she's seeing anyone?"

Oh goody. We're not finished talking about me yet. And it definitely seems as if the conversation is about to get even more uncomfortable.

The server comes to take our order, and I think I'm saved from having to answer Dad's question, but he still has an expectant glint in his eyes after she leaves.

I'm not off the hook.

And tragically, there's still no mimosa sitting in front of me.

"I don't think Charlotte's ready to date quite yet." I force myself to meet his gaze and do my best to pretend we're talking about someone else—some pathetic, wounded girl who isn't me.

"I still don't understand what went wrong between her and Adam. She seemed so happy." Susan sighs. "Do you have any idea? She never explained it to us."

Of course I didn't. I was too raw. Too humiliated. "I don't know the specifics. But she made it clear he wasn't the right man for her."

My father snorted. "It would've been nice if she'd figured that out a little sooner."

I reach for my water glass. It trembles slightly in my hand, and I take a sip.

Susan fills the dead air by reminding me that the wedding invitations had already been sent out when I called everything off. We'd spent weeks returning gifts and writing apology notes. She says all of this as if I hadn't been there, as if I hadn't been forced to write the words *I'm sorry* over and over again when Adam was the one who should have been apologizing.

But no.

The decision to cancel the wedding was mine, and that made me the bad guy. Setting the record straight wasn't an option. Ginny would have been crushed if she'd known she had any part of my breakup. I couldn't put her through that. I'd been heartbroken enough for the both of us.

"Charlotte doesn't like talking about all of this," I say. "So it hasn't really come up lately."

"Of course it hasn't. We just worry about her sometimes." Susan gives my hand a pat. "That's why we're asking you about it instead of her. The poor dear."

Poor dear?

My mimosa finally arrives and I grab hold of it like Hermione Granger reaching for a book of spells.

I'd like to blame the alcohol for what comes out of my mouth next, but since I've only taken a sip—more like a gulp, really—I can't. My words are deliberate, and I'm completely sober. "Actually, she *is* sort of seeing someone."

Dad drops his fork. Susan's eyes go comically wide.

I take a furious sip of my drink. Is it really so hard to believe that I have a secret boyfriend?

My father retrieves his rogue cutlery and narrows his gaze. "I don't understand. Why hasn't she said anything?"

"Maybe it's someone we know," Susan suggests. Her hand flutters to her chest. "Oh, is it Adam? Are they back together?"

I nearly gag. "Gross. No."

Dad frowns. "Who then?"

"Someone much better than Adam. More attractive in every possible way. Kinder. Smarter. Unbelievably charming." I let out a wistful sigh, because yes, I'm thinking about my clandestine meetings with a certain dreamy pageant judge. "It's a secret, though. So you can't say anything about it. Not a word. Charlotte would kill me if she knew I'd mentioned it."

"If he's so perfect, why is he a secret?" Dad says flatly.

He doesn't believe me. Of course he doesn't, because we're talking about me. The *poor dear*. I could probably tell him that Ginny had seven secret boyfriends—a different one for every day of the week—and he'd believe me in a heartbeat.

I grit my teeth. "It's new. She doesn't want to rush things."

Also, he's not technically her secret boyfriend.

It's clearly wishful thinking. Gray sent me champagne and we kissed. Once. He's definitely a secret, but the boyfriend part is iffy at best . . .

And there's still the inconvenient truth of my actual identity.

Who am I kidding? Gray definitely isn't my secret boyfriend. He *can't* be. I'd have to be an idiot to even speak to him again. The smartest thing to do would be to stay as far away from him as possible.

But that's impossible. *Literally.* Because when I look up from my empty mimosa glass, he's standing right there.

I blink, convinced I'm hallucinating.

"Miss Texas." He smiles. "Good morning."

My stomach flips. My heart hammers in my chest. Everything about this encounter seems real. Just in case, I glance at Dad and Susan. Both of their gazes are fixed on Gray.

It's really him. And we're really speaking. Right here, out in the open.

"Good morning." I smile back.

"Hello." He offers his hand to my father. "I'm Gray Beckham, one of the pageant judges."

Dad stands and shakes Gray's hand. "Henry Gorman. Nice to meet you. I'm Ginny's father, and this is my wife, Susan."

Susan stands, and it feels really strange to be the only one still seated, so I stand too. My hand brushes against Gray's as I rise to my feet, sending a cascade of goose bumps up and down my arm.

"It's nice of you to come and support your daughter," he says.

It takes every bit of willpower I can muster not to look at him. Because if I do, I'll probably grin like a love-struck teenager and everyone will know that I've got feelings for him. And no one can know that, least of all Gray.

But he's not looking at me either, and it feels deliberate. Necessary, even. The fact that our eyes don't meet seems far more meaningful than any actual eye contact.

"We wouldn't miss it." Susan smiles.

Dad nods. "We're very proud."

"We know we can't attend the rest of the preliminaries, but we thought it would be nice to come a little early because Ginny's . . ."

I lurch forward, stumbling toward Susan as if I'm about to strangle her, or more accurately, clamp my hand over her mouth. She's about to mention Ginny's twin. *Me.* And Gray can't know that I exist.

"Whoa." He reaches for me, slipping an arm around my

waist and righting me before I crash into my stepmother. "Are you okay?"

"So sorry." I gesture toward my pageant stilts. "It's these heels. I'm still not quite used to them, I guess. I'm fine."

I'm *not* fine.

That was a close call. Too close. My nerves are all tangled up in knots. But somewhere beneath the swirl of panic, I'm also hyperaware of Gray's hands on me. His fingertips rest just a second too long on my hip—a second in which I practically melt into a puddle at his feet.

You're avoiding him now, remember?

Right. That's the plan. As plans go, it's a very good one. A smart one. A *mandatory* one. I'm just not sure I can actually follow through with it.

"Are you steady now?" He crosses his arms, and I pretend it's his way of stopping himself from touching me again. Judging by the suddenly firm set of his jaw, that might actually be the case.

"Steady as a rock." Another lie. I'm weak in the knees.

I clear my throat, ready to thank Gray for stopping by and insist that he move along because we shouldn't monopolize his time. After all, there are forty-nine other contestants who'd probably love to chat him up over brunch.

But before I can say anything, he turns toward my dad and resumes their previous conversation.

I wrap my arms around myself, trying my best to hold it together. I'm on high alert, ready to cause another awkward distraction if the discussion veers anywhere near identical-twins territory.

"I'm sorry the prelims aren't open to the public, but there are a lot of great things to do around here. The resort has all kinds of amenities, like golf and tennis. Plus there's the spa." Gray clears his throat, and his gaze flits toward mine. Just for a second. Just quickly enough for me to know that it was intentional. "The swan boats are lovely. It would be nice to take one out for a paddle around the lake sometime. In the moonlight maybe."

Gray shifts his weight from one foot to the other. When his arm brushes against mine, he doesn't pull away. Neither do I.

To the outside world, it probably looks like nothing. Just two people standing side by side. But the innocent contact is enough to make my cheeks warm. I feel lovely and floaty, as though I've been drinking the champagne he sent to my room last night.

Gray flashes a grin at my parents. "Just a thought." Then his gaze collides with mine. And holds. "Tonight would be nice."

I blink.

Am I hearing things, or did he just ask me out on a secret date?

No, surely not. He was merely making small talk with my parents. Wasn't he?

Of course. That's exactly what he was doing. And yet . . .

Why do I know that if I show up at the swan boats tonight after the evening gown competition, I'll find Gray Beckham waiting for me?

My dad nods. "We'll certainly give that some consideration, although Susan doesn't swim so we tend to stay away from boats."

"That's a shame. I think there's supposed to be a full moon tonight. It would be lovely." He glances at me again, and that's when I'm sure. He's definitely sending me some sort of secret signal. "Maybe a stroll around the resort instead."

My father says something in response. I have no idea what it is. The conversation becomes nothing but background noise because my thoughts are screaming things about a secret date, the swan boats, and a full moon. Gray's words are running through my head in a heavenly, continuous loop.

Tonight would be nice . . .

It would be lovely.

It *would* be lovely. It would also be dangerous and borderline insane.

I can't show up at the swan boats. I know that. But I also know that I will, and as much as I'd love to blame this potentially self-destructive act on the mysterious forces of the full moon, it wouldn't be fair. Nor would it be fair to blame my parents and their humiliating assessment of my plunge into solitude following my breakup with Adam.

The choice is mine, and mine alone. And even though I know I should barricade myself in my hotel room with Ginny, I won't. Because I want this—more than I've wanted anything in such a long time. I want *him*.

And this little rendezvous he's hinting at is something I can't resist, because it's not an accidental meeting in the stairwell or a chance encounter in the ice closet. It's not me throwing myself at him again and catching him unaware. Quite the opposite. It's steeped in intention, which can only mean one thing.

He wants me too.

Maybe there's a way this won't end in disaster. It's possible, isn't it? It has to be, although I can't see how. I'm at a crossroads. At some point, I'm going to have to choose between myself and my twin. Between my dreams and hers.

"Nice to meet you both," Gray says to my dad and Susan, dragging my thoughts back to the present. Before he leaves, he turns toward me. "Best of luck, Miss Texas. I'll see you later?"

Later, as in onstage in the evening-gown competition? Or later tonight, in a swan boat beneath a moonlit sky?

Either way, my answer is the same.

"You certainly will."

16

I spend the majority of the day preparing for the evening-gown competition, which is set to begin at six o'clock.

Ginny assures me it's the easiest of all the prelims. I'm not required to say anything, twirl anything, or bare any part of my body that hasn't been seen in public since I was a small child. All I have to do is glide up and down the runway in a fabulous gown. No problem, I think.

Naturally, I'm wrong.

First, Ginny informs me that I can't wear the pageant shoes I've finally managed to master. Mostly. I still live in fear that I'll tumble off them and fall to my death in a bedazzled pile of glitter, chiffon, and chandelier earrings. But my feet haven't actively bled in twenty-four hours, which sadly, is a major win.

"I don't get it. Why can't I wear these?" I say, stepping down from my nude patent leather frenemies.

"The heel isn't high enough. The gown is long. You need another inch of platform. Minimum." She hands me a silver sparkly pair of platform stilettos nearly identical in style to the ones I've just discarded.

But the new ones are definitely taller. "If I put these on, my updo will be in danger of hitting the ceiling."

I'm only half joking. As soon as I returned from my awkward breakfast, Ginny sat me down and got to work on my hair. Countless bobby pins and a full can of hair spray later, I'm sporting an artfully created ballerina bun that somehow manages to look glamorous and a little bit messy all at the same time. Ginny calls this look "elegantly just got out of bed," and even though the description might be the dumbest thing I've ever heard, I get the reference. I look like a woman in a perfume ad—barefoot in a ball gown, accompanied by a George Clooney look-alike in a tuxedo with his bow tie hanging loose around his neck.

I wonder idly if any of the beautiful couples in those advertisements ever got busy in a small, paddle-powered watercraft. You know, swan boat and chill.

"Your face is beet red." Ginny frowns at me. "And the skin on your chest is all splotchy, like it gets when you're anxious. What's wrong with you?"

I'm terrified, that's what's wrong with me.

It's been a while since I've been intimate with a man. A long while. After Adam and I broke up, I spent months

Kent Libraries,
Registration and Archives

www.kent.gov.uk/libraries
Tel: 03000 41 31 31

Borrowed items 16/03/2020 11:11

XXXXXXX8103

Item Title	Due Date
The accidental beauty Queen	06/04/2020

- Indicates items borrowed today

Thank you for using self service

wondering if he'd been pretending I was Ginny every time we made love. The thought filled me with such shame and loathing that I completely shut down in the intimacy department. It's been months since I've let myself contemplate kissing a man, much less getting undressed in front of one.

Until yesterday in the ice closet, anyway.

Now I'm contemplating doing all sorts of things with Gray. Something about him makes me feel safe. It doesn't make sense, particularly since he thinks I'm my sister.

But somehow he also seems to see through the charade. He noticed me when I was still Charlotte. Every time I close my eyes, I see the way he looked at me in the stairwell on that very first night.

Later, Hermione.

Those words, coupled with the appreciation in his gaze when he said them, make me believe I can do this. I can trust Gray Beckham.

Can't I?

"No." Ginny meets my gaze in the full-length mirror on the back of our bathroom door and shakes her head.

"What do you mean 'no'?" I say quietly.

"This dress." She aims a critical gaze at the crimson mermaid-style gown I've somehow managed to squeeze into. Ginny had it custom made especially for the Miss American Treasure pageant. "It's all wrong."

I agree. I feel like a bad Jessica Rabbit impersonator. The

gown isn't me at all . . . but since when does that matter? For the most part, Charlotte Gorman has ceased to exist.

"Maybe it will look better once I put on the shoes," I say.

It can't hurt. The hem of the dress is pooled on the floor. If I try to take a step, I'll surely trip over a mass of red velvet.

"Nope. It's just not right on you." Ginny unzips the back of the gown. "Take it off. I've got a few other options we can try."

I step out of the gown while she pulls an assortment of glittering frocks from the closet. One by one, I try them on. First up is an off-the-shoulder violet gown, with a voluminous tiered skirt that swallows me whole. There's no way I could walk in this thing, much less glide. I'd get all tangled up in the skirt in a matter of seconds.

Ginny crosses her arms. "Next."

I wiggle into a white beaded sheath dress that would probably look sophisticated on Ginny, but again makes me feel like a child playing dress-up. My sister sighs and points to the pile of dresses on the bed.

The next one is covered in feathers that tickle my nose. I sneeze four times in rapid succession. I take it off without bothering to wait for Ginny's opinion. It'll never work.

"How many evening gowns did you bring?" I ask as she pulls another one from the stack.

She narrows her gaze at the dress in her arms and flings it back onto the bed.

"That's a lot of gowns."

"It's always good to have extras. In pageantry, you have to be prepared for the unexpected—spills, split seams, and all that."

"Does it really matter?" I glance at the digital clock on the nightstand. We're running out of time. Believe it or not, this impromptu fashion show is taking hours. "Didn't you say I'm pretty much a lock for the finals since I won the talent competition?"

She gives me an odd look, and I correct myself. "I mean *you're* a lock for the finals."

Sometimes I forget I'm not in this for the long haul. There's only one preliminary event left after the evening-gown competition tonight. Tomorrow afternoon is the onstage-question portion of the pageant prelims. Each contestant will reach into an acrylic box and choose a question at random. She'll then have two minutes to articulate a coherent response. All of this takes place on the fly, with zero preparation time. The question is read aloud and boom, the clock starts ticking.

Ginny might be better by tomorrow. It's hard to say. Most of the lingering swelling in her face is a result of the nose injury I inflicted during my ill-fated baton lesson. Last night, she spent an hour in front of the mirror with a makeup brush and three different shades of contouring powder in an effort to slim down the damage. It didn't end well.

But I know without a doubt that when the finals roll around, I'm out. There's a rest day between the end of the prelims and the finals, followed by an entire day of rehearsal for the big production numbers that take place during the televised pageant finals. Think Sandra Bullock dressed as the Statue of Liberty in *Miss Congeniality*.

In short, my twin still has two and a half days before she takes the stage in the finals. She'll be ready, come hell or high water.

"You can't think that way," she says. "The talent win definitely helps. But making the finals is never a certainty. At this point, you could still get knocked into the bottom half. It would just take something really big."

Like being exposed as an imposter. Or getting caught in flagrante delicto with one of the pageant judges in a swan boat.

"We need to find a dress." I swallow. The evening gown suddenly seems vitally important, not only to my success in the prelims, but to my very survival.

"Oh, wait! I think I've got just the thing." Ginny brightens and makes a mad dash for her suitcase. "It's a gorgeous dress. I've been dragging it around from one pageant to the next, but I've never worn it because it's not really my taste."

She's rummaging through the bag, tossing things aside. I'm pretty sure I see a one-piece swimsuit fly through the air, contrary to Ginny's insistence that she only packed bikinis. It takes monumental self-restraint not to bring attention to her blatant lie, but I manage to keep my mouth shut. After all, I haven't exactly been a pillar of honesty lately.

"Ah! Found it." Ginny lets out a little squeal as she pulls mile after mile of sheer pink organza from the suitcase.

I'm skeptical. It's a lot of fabric, and despite the volume of all that chiffon, it doesn't seem to actually cover anything. I can see every detail of Ginny's hands straight through it, including her pastel lavender manicure.

"Don't give me that look." She holds up the top of the gown, and it's undeniably gorgeous. The delicate chiffon is gathered in a diagonal ruching pattern, allowing the faintest glimpse of the structured corset beneath. "The corset is fully lined. I'm not going to send you down the runway naked. Trust me."

Trust me.

I've heard that a lot this week, and somehow I feel less inclined to put my blind faith in my twin right now than I did a few days ago. But what choice do I have?

I hold out my hand. "Give it to me. I'll try it on."

This time, my sister is right.

The gown isn't at all similar to any of Ginny's other dresses. Actually, I've never seen anything like it. Ever. Which is pretty remarkable considering I've spent most of my life beauty pageant-adjacent.

"This is . . ." I shake my head, unable to continue. The pink gown is *special*. Its innocent color, combined with a thick layer of handcrafted flowery tulle rosettes along the hem makes the chiffon's sheerness seem sweet rather than sultry. I feel like I'm wearing something made of spun sugar. I feel . . . beautiful. And yet, somehow, like Charlotte instead of Ginny.

"I don't know what to say." I press my fingertips to my mouth so Ginny can't see the tremble in my lower lip. This isn't like me. I don't get emotional over fashion. Unlike most brides, I didn't shed a tear when I tried on my wedding gown.

But this feels different. I'm not sure why, but it does. A lump has lodged itself in my throat and my hands are shaking. I want to take this feeling and bottle it, so that when this charade is over and everything falls apart, I can remember that I didn't just do it for Ginny. I also did it for me, and there were moments it was worth it—in spite of whatever reckoning is coming my way.

"Keep it," Ginny whispers.

"What? Why?"

"Because it looks like it was made for you. It's beautiful, but it's not right for me. I look like I'm trying too hard when I put it on. On you, it's perfect." She smiles.

I catch her gaze in the mirror and for a second, it looks like she might cry. "You look stunning as hell and at the same time, sweet like cotton candy. All sugar and spice and everything nice."

If she only knew.

✕✕

The evening-gown competition passes in a blur. I don't win, but I feel magnificent onstage. The pink chiffon swishes around my legs, soft as rose petals, and for once, I have no trouble whatsoever making eye contact with Gray as he sits at the judges' table.

He freezes when he sees me. The air between us is electric, and every muscle in his body goes tight. Rigid. He doesn't even write down a score in his binder until the judge beside him prods him to do so.

I suck in a breath, do my final twirl, and glide toward the stage exit.

Don't look back.

My fingernails dig into my palms.

Don't do it.

I look. The expression I'm aiming for is a coy peek over my shoulder, one last smile for the audience. But my gaze flits immediately to Gray. He's the only judge still watching me. All the others are sitting with their heads bent, scribbling on the pages of their judge's books. The last thing I see before I disappear behind the thick velvet curtain is the corner of his mouth quirking into a secret smile.

This is a dangerous game we're playing.

Someone is going to notice all our subtle communication. Whether it's my parents, the judges, the Miss American Treasure officials, or one of the pageant girls, it's going to happen . . . unless I put a stop to things and quit before someone gets hurt.

The trouble is, even if I cut off all communication with Gray, someone *will* get hurt.

And that someone is me.

I'm breathless by the time I take my place in the wings and watch the last contestants take the stage. Only seven states remain. While they float before the judging panel in a variety of beaded, bedazzled, bespoke gowns, I try and force myself to believe whatever is happening between Gray and me is harmless.

But it's not.

As much as I want to believe we're not hurting anyone, we are. This pageant is important to a lot of people, and now that I've experienced it myself—now that I've gotten to know these women—I can't dismiss it quite as easily as I used to.

But I'm not *really* cheating, am I? And Gray and I are consenting adults. My attraction to him has nothing to do with the pageant. I'm certainly not planning on meeting him at the swan boats because I'm angling for a higher score.

Somehow I doubt my fellow contestants would see it that way.

Fellow *contestants? Oh, so now you're actually one of them?*

The exquisite dress I'm wearing is going to my head. I'm just a temporary substitute. None of this is real. Why can't I seem to remember that?

"You look amazing," Lisa Ng says to me while we're in the wings. "You're a shoo-in for finals."

"Thank you." I beam. "So are you."

She gives me a hug. Everywhere I turn, girls are embracing one another, and even though everything I'm wearing right now is borrowed—the sash, the gown, the shoes, and in a way, even the face—this moment is mine. It belongs to me and it feels as real as the pounding of my heart does when I slip out of the ballroom and push through the resort's glass double doors, onto the veranda.

Back in our hotel room, my twin is waiting for me to return and give her the play-by-play of the evening-gown competition. Dad and Susan are probably there too. They want to take us out for dinner tonight someplace festive. I haven't bothered to make another excuse why Ginny and I can't be seen together, because I'm going to be a no-show.

I have no idea how I'll explain my absence. I can't think about that right now. My twin and our misguided charade is the furthest thing from my mind while I tiptoe through the moonlight toward the swan boats. I am a Brontë heroine, caught in a moment of weakness, stumbling toward a hopeless mistake.

A sultry breeze rustles the palm trees and whips my diaphanous gown so that the skirt floats behind me like a dandelion puff.

Make a wish.

I do. And when I reach the faraway dock, my wish is there, waiting for me with a smile on his lips and a look in his eyes I know I'll never forget. It's a look of reverence. Of pure, unabashed longing. It's the way that Heathcliff probably looked at Catherine on the windswept moors, minus all the brooding and tragic revenge.

"You came," he says quietly.

"I did."

He comes closer to cup my face in his warm hands and rest his forehead against mine. My pulse is racing, and when Gray brushes the pad of his thumb along my lower lip, my breath catches.

"What are we doing, Hermione?" he whispers.

If he'd called me Miss Texas, I might have been capable

of walking away. But he didn't. He called me the name that can only belong to me, and so I stay. I stay, and I don't wait for him to take the lead. I'm tired of waiting, tired of holding back, tired of hiding all the time.

"We're making magic," I say, and then my mouth is on his and his hands are in my hair and he's kissing me with a passion I've never known before.

It's raw, aching, and honest. And even though this man doesn't even know my name, I've never been more myself, more genuine. I'm still not Meg March or Jane Bennet. I'll always be a Jo or a Lizzie, no matter what kind of dress I wear or how I style my hair. But that's okay, because for once, I feel like the heroine of my own story.

It's taken pretending to be someone else to make me realize who I actually am. And when I give myself to him, I'm no longer trapped in that blurry place where I'm never sure where Ginny stops and I begin.

It's only me.

I am myself.

And for tonight, I am his.

17

By the time I return to our hotel room, the resort is no longer bathed in moonlight. The sun is rising over the misty pink horizon, making the swan boats in the lake look as if they're floating on flames rather than water.

I have no idea what time it is. My phone is back in the room, along with the rest of my possessions. But the hotel staff is already setting up for breakfast on the outdoor patio where I had brunch with my parents yesterday, and the emerald lawn that lies beyond the palm trees is dotted with golfers.

I've been out all night.

How is that possible? It feels as though I just walked out of the ballroom and into Gray's arms.

A lot has happened since then, and the memory of the majority of it makes me blush pinker than the train of the chiffon dress that trails behind me on the lush green grass. There were sweet moments too. Hours, actually . . . hours in which Gray held me close and we talked about anything and everything and I laughed until my cheeks hurt.

Gray still doesn't know the truth about who I am. But he knows all about my mom, and he knows that I was engaged a year ago and I called off the wedding after my fiancé admitted he had feelings for my sister. He knows the names of all my favorite books, and I know his. He loves John Steinbeck and Ursula Le Guin, and when he was in sixth-grade English class, he broke down in tears reading *Where the Red Fern Grows*. I know that he drove his sister to all her chemotherapy appointments and he was there, holding her hand, when she died. I know little things too, like how he hates avocados and that if he were on death row and had to choose his final meal, it would be a bowl of ramen from a little place in Tokyo where he always goes when he's in Japan for the World Science and Technology Conference.

We've exchanged more than kisses, and after I left him, I'm holding on tight to everything he's told me, every kiss, every quickened breath. I'm brimming with memories, and I don't need to catch a glimpse of my reflection in the hotel's glass double doors to know that I look like a woman who's been thoroughly ravished.

But I do, and what I see gives me pause. Yes, I'm clearly a pageant girl on a walk of shame. My fancy updo is nothing but a memory, my eyeliner is smudged into dark half-moons beneath my eyes and my silver shoes dangle from my fingertips while I tiptoe on bare feet. But beyond the obvious, I see something else. There's fire in my eyes and my lips are bee-stung, swollen with kisses. I look like a poem—something penned by Wordsworth, all dancing daffodils and smokeless air.

I look like a woman in love.

Maybe I am, I think as I slip into the hotel and pad toward the stairwell. I must be, because for once the idea doesn't frighten me. Even though right here, right now, it should. It should scare the life out of me.

Once I'm upstairs and standing outside of the room Ginny and I have been sharing for the past week, I realize I've lost my key. It might be in the ballroom, where later today, the onstage-question portion of the pageant will determine the finalists. Or it could be in a swan boat, discarded along with my inhibitions and any sense of self-preservation I once possessed. Either way, I'm locked out, so I take a deep breath and knock on the door.

Time to face the music.

I'm not sure what exactly awaits me on the other side of the door, but I'm prepared for drama. Worry, anger, tears— these are all very real possibilities. Ginny had been furious with me for staying too long at the party the other night, but this is a whole new level of abandon. I deserve whatever I've got coming to me. If Ginny had stayed out all night without giving me a heads-up, I'd definitely be upset.

But the door swings open to reveal a sight I am in no way prepared for.

"Hey." Ginny sweeps me with her gaze, and her reaction to my disheveled appearance is nothing more than a flippant shrug. "Come on in. I'm busy getting ready."

I don't need to ask my twin what she's getting ready *for*, because her plans are obvious. She's shed her ubiquitous terry cloth robe and slipper socks and is now dressed in one of the evening gowns I tried on the night before. It's the red one—the Jessica Rabbit gown—but instead of looking like an over-the-top Halloween costume like it did when I tried it on, it looks flipping amazing.

Ginny's waist is smaller than I've ever seen it. I'm not sure how it's possible, but she somehow seems to be both thinner than I am and curvier at the same time. My mind goes instantly to a place where I never allow it to wander—straight to the bikini photos on her Instagram. The ones Adam bookmarked so he could pore over them again and again.

I swallow hard. There's obviously something far more important happening right now than my humiliating relationship flashbacks. My twin is in pageant mode.

"Um." My pulse pounds so hard, I feel as if I'm choking on my heartbeat. "What's going on?"

"This." Ginny turns away from the mirror and waves a slender hand at her face. "I'm better! Not all the way back to normal, but close enough. God, just in the nick of time.

Great effort, by the way. But I've got it from here. I know how to win."

I wait for her to acknowledge the fact that I'm still wearing my gown from the night before or that I've been out all night . . . or even that I've lost my key to the room.

She doesn't. She just turns back toward the mirror and resumes curling her eyelashes.

I don't know why I'm surprised. My role in this pageant was just a walk-on, and now it's ended. I'm no longer needed. So what difference does it make where I've been or who I might have been with.

Ginny shoots me another glance in the mirror. "What are you doing? Take that dress off. I thought you'd be practically ripping it off to get back into your nerdy T-shirts and boyfriend jeans."

She's right. I should be relieved. I never wanted any of this to begin with, and I knew better than to think that I'd be the one with a glittering tiara on her head when all was said and done.

But I'm not. My knees wobble, and I have the strangest sensation that my body is on the verge of collapsing in on itself. I take a deep inhale, and I have to concentrate hard on the simple act of breathing in and out.

I'm familiar with this feeling. I'm sorry to say I know it well.

Humiliation.

I wrap my arms around myself and stare at my twin's flawless reflection. Her makeup is perfect, and her hair hangs in a glossy curtain down her back. Even though she just said her face isn't "all the way back to normal," I see no trace whatsoever of the swelling she's been battling all week. She's a vision.

And then my gaze shifts ever so slightly to the left, and I see myself standing in the background. I no longer look like the wild, romantic goddess I fancied myself just moments ago. I'm a mess. My gown has held up surprisingly well, but Ginny's fits her like a glove. We're twins. Identical in every way. But we look like before and after photos of the same person. And just like always, I'm cast in the role of *before*.

Ginny glances over her shoulder at me as she dabs her lips with gloss. "Take off the sash, would you? I'm going to need it."

That's what does it. Those words, which she's so carelessly tossed out, are the final straw. My sister *still* hasn't asked where I've been. She hasn't even thanked me for getting her this far. Instead of gratitude, I'm being ordered to take off the sash.

An eerie calm comes over me as the heat of my humiliation cools into rage. Wordlessly, I slip the Miss Texas sash over my head. Then I carry it with me as I cross toward the vanity. Ginny turns and holds out her palms, clearly expecting me to hand it over. Instead, I reach behind her to pick up the tiny scissors she uses to trim her false eyelashes to the proper dimensions.

Then I cut the sash right down the middle.

Ginny lets out a horrific gasp as the *Miss* half falls to the floor. I hand her the part that says *Texas* and she takes it as if in a daze.

When I stomp toward the closet for my suitcase, I spot Buttercup watching me. Her eyes are even bigger and rounder than they usually are. I've managed to shock even the dog.

"What have you done?" Ginny says in a wooden voice. Then again—louder, with more than a touch of hysteria. *"What have you done?"*

I toss my suitcase onto the bed, undo the zipper, and flop it open. Buttercup immediately scrambles inside, which takes the edge off my fury. The little Frenchie sleeps on my bed instead of Ginny's, and now she's trying to stow away in my luggage.

I decide I'm taking her home with me. I don't care what Ginny has to say about it. Besides, my rap sheet is pretty long now. I've impersonated my sister and cheated in a national pageant. I may as well add dognapping to my list of crimes.

"Hey." Ginny pokes me in the center of my back with such force that I nearly fall face-first onto the bed. "I asked you a question."

I spin around. "You want to know what I've done? Fine. I'll tell you. First, I let you talk me into impersonating you in this pageant. I let you make me over so I looked like you. I changed everything about myself so I could help you achieve your dream. *I got you to the finals*, and now you're acting like it's nothing."

I also slept with one of the judges, but now probably isn't the time to bring up that little tidbit.

She lifts a brow. "I'm not in the finals yet. The onstage questions are this afternoon, remember?"

Seriously?

"Whatever. I also took care of your dog all week, so guess what? She's my dog now."

Ginny looks at Buttercup and then back at me. "What in the world has gotten into you?"

"Listen to yourself. Do you have any idea how self-centered you sound?" I cross my arms. "I've been out all night, and you haven't said a word about it. Did you even notice?"

"All night?" For the first time since my return, she looks at me. *Really* looks. "I thought you just stayed out really late and got in after I went to bed. I assumed you were off celebrating with the other girls and then darted out again this morning."

"In my evening gown?" I roll my eyes. I'm right. She has been looking right through me all along. "Tell me, Ginny. What do you see when you look at me? Do you see an actual person? Your twin? Or do you only see a less attractive reflection of yourself?"

It's harsh. I know it is. But I can't seem to stop the ugliness from spewing out of my mouth. I've been too silent for too long.

"Are you kidding right now? Of course I see you." She takes a closer look at me and her gaze narrows. Finally. She recognizes my messy state for what it is.

Who is he?

I can see the question shining in her eyes. She desperately wants to ask me, but she knows I won't tell her. Not mid-rant.

So instead she clears her throat, and in her best pageant-girl, world-peace-loving voice she calmly says, "Thank you for taking my place. I'm more grateful than you know. How can I repay you?"

"Let me keep going." The words are out of my mouth before I can stop them.

She blinks. "What do you mean?"

But she knows. She just can't believe it's what I want.

Neither can I, actually. "Let me continue in the pageant. I started it, I want to finish it."

For a long, loaded moment, neither of us says a word. I know better than to hope that she'll agree. I'm not even sure why I want her to.

Yes, you do, a tiny voice whispers inside my head. *You're afraid of disappearing again.*

"No." Ginny shakes her head. Her gaze is as hard as stone. "Anything but that. You know how important this pageant is to me."

"She was my mother too," I say. "Besides, you owe me."

I should stop. I *need* to stop. The dam has broken and soon I'm going to say something I won't be able to take back.

"What do you mean, I owe you? What for? The pageant?" Ginny sighs. She doesn't have a clue.

So after keeping the truth to myself for more than a year, I finally enlighten her.

"For Adam," I say flatly.

Ginny's mouth opens and then closes. I watch as she tries to process what I've just said. The air between us swirls with ugly truths and secrets, swollen from being held too tightly for far too long.

Slowly, every drop of color drains from Ginny's face. She shakes her head. Her eyes are full of questions, and I can tell she doesn't know what I'm talking about, but she knows it's bad.

I want to swallow my words. I never wanted to hurt her. Not like this.

What's *wrong* with me?

I thought I had a handle on things. Just last night, everything had seemed so clear. So wonderful. And now . . .

Now my twin is looking at me, and she's seeing me. *Really* seeing me, and I'm ashamed.

"Tell me," she whispers.

There's an awful, aching pain in her voice, and I hate that I've put it there. Intellectually, I know it was really Adam's doing, not mine. But my heart tells me otherwise.

I should have told her long ago. If I had, it wouldn't have slipped out like this. I wouldn't have hurled it at her like a weapon. But now I have, and there's no going back.

"Tell me," she says again. "Please."

So I do.

I tell her everything, starting with the sinking feeling I had on the cruise, right on up to the conversation I overheard between Adam and his best man.

"He said he hoped he could 'trade up.'" I drop my gaze. I can't look her in the eye and say these things. "When his friend asked what he meant, Adam admitted the only reason he wanted to marry me was so he could spend more time with you. He hoped that once you got to know him, you'd fall in love with him and then you two could ride off into the sunset together." Leaving me behind. Alone. No husband, no twin. Just me.

Ginny looks as though she might gag. She actually has a hard time swallowing before she can speak again. "That's disgusting. And completely insane. I would *never* do that to you. Surely you know that."

"I do, but that doesn't make it hurt any less." I nod.

How am I having this conversation? Why am I not crying? I should be falling apart right now. Instead, I feel hollow. Numb.

"I think deep down, Adam knew it too. But if he married me, he was still getting the next best thing."

Ginny shakes her head. "Don't say that. You're not the next best thing. We're twins, but we're also individual people. You deserve better than that."

Do I?

I think about Gray and the fact that I still haven't managed to tell him the truth about who I am. The only thing I know with any certainty right now is that *he* deserves better.

Better than me. That's a fact.

"Why didn't you say anything? I don't understand." Ginny takes a deep, shuddering inhale. Then she frowns, and asks the one question I fear most. "Why are you telling me this now, after all this time?"

Because sometimes you act as if I am second best.

I can't say it, and at last I know why . . .

Because I've let her treat me that way. I've let her do it because I believed it myself.

Not anymore, though. I am no longer Ginny's substitute. I'm not her shadow, nor am I the runner-up in our own private, twisted version of a beauty pageant. I am my own person. Charlotte Gorman.

I just wish I liked Charlotte as much as I used to.

18

After our argument, Ginny quietly resumes getting ready for the onstage-question portion of the prelims. Neither one of us says a word about whether I'll remain in the pageant. I'm finished.

Truthfully, I no longer want to do it. I just want to get as far away from this mess as I can. The only thing stopping me from gathering Buttercup into my arms and running out the door is Gray.

I can't leave without saying goodbye . . . without telling him the truth and explaining why I've let my lie get so out of hand. I have no idea when I'll get to talk to him or what I'll say. But *I'm sorry* is probably a pretty good starting point.

I fold my things and place them into my suitcase, one at a time. I don't have the heart to make Buttercup move, so I pile my things up around her while she curls into a ball and snores. Eventually, I'll drag her out of my bag, but I can't do it yet. I can't bear to disappoint her. I've let down enough people already, myself included.

I set aside a plain black T-shirt and jeans for the trip back to Dallas, and when I slip into the bathroom to shed my evening gown and get dressed, I hear the door to our room click firmly shut.

And then nothing. Just a deafening quiet.

Sure enough, when I exit the bathroom, my twin is gone. Ginny is actually going through with it. She's going to climb up on that stage and pretend she's been the one competing in the pageant all along.

I shake my head. Why am I so surprised? She's been primping all morning. Clearly she's intent on winning the crown.

I guess I thought that our conversation might have made her realize how foolish our charade has been. Granted, we veered way off topic when I lobbed the conversational hand grenade of Adam into the mix. But couldn't she see that what we've done is wrong? I don't deserve to walk away from this week with a glittering tiara on my head, but neither does she.

I sit for a minute, trying to figure out my next move. I know what it is, though. Deep down, I've known all along.

I've got to find Gray.

Leaving the room is risky, but I don't have a choice. I stick to the stairwell until I reach the first floor. Then I creep toward the bustling hallway that leads toward the ballroom.

It's a hive of activity. I've lost all track of time, and apparently, the onstage-question competition is due to start any minute. I have to get out of here before someone spots me. I'll just have to talk to Gray later.

But when I turn to go, I see him. He's at the far end of the hallway, opposite me. And he's not alone.

He's talking to my sister.

All the breath leaves my body in a single, nauseating whoosh. I can't see the two of them together. Not now. Not when the memory of my night with Gray is still wrapped around my heart like its own beauty queen sash. And not when I've just had to confront all of the pain of Adam's betrayal with such brutal, aching honesty.

Ginny still has no idea that Gray is anyone other than a member of the judging panel. But Gray will take one look at her and think she's me.

He won't do anything outwardly demonstrative, like kiss her. He won't even touch her. But he'll look at her the same way he looked at me last night when I first walked onto the dock. That look means too much to me to watch him bestow it on my sister. I know it's a far different thing than what Adam did to me. I shouldn't even compare the two.

But it aches in the same brutal way.

So I turn around and flee.

I don't think about where I'm going or who might see me. I just want to put as much distance between myself and the Gray/Ginny encounter as I possibly can.

My inattentiveness comes back to bite me in the end, because just as I round the corner of the hotel's palatial lobby, I run smack into my parents.

"Whoa there," my dad says as he catches me by the shoulders. "Where's the fire, Charlotte?"

I stare at him for a beat, wondering if he would have any idea who I am if I wasn't dressed in my regular clothes, which I've started to think of as "the Charlotte costume." Or more precisely, the kind of thing someone wears when they don't care very much about personal appearance.

"Hi," I say stiffly.

He wraps me into a big bear hug, and I feel my resentment melt away. I can't be mad at my father. He loves me, and I love him right back. Other than Ginny, he's been the most constant presence in my life. I *need* him.

Especially now.

I cling to him like a small child and close my eyes, wishing with all my might that there was something he could say or do to make it all better. But he can't tuck me into the corner of his office anymore with a book to take away my troubles. I'm a grown up, and this is an adult-size mess I've made. For once in my life, a book can't fix things.

"Hey, what is it?" He holds me at arm's length and studies me, probably thinking I've had some sort of falling out with my "secret boyfriend."

Nope. Not yet, anyway.

"Nothing." I paste on a smile.

"Good." He nods. "Because we just got word that the pageant has opened up today's prelim to family members. We're on our way to go watch your sister compete."

I shake my head. "But the prelims are supposed to be private. Are you sure?"

Susan nods. "Absolutely. It's all over the Miss American Treasure Facebook page. A small audience will give the girls more practice for when they have to face the onstage question during the finals. They're expecting a sold-out crowd, not to mention all the people who will be watching at home on television."

"Right." Oh God. I can flee Orlando on the next plane out of here, but the pageant is still going to be televised. There's no escaping it. It will be a trending topic on Twitter, and every talk show in America will chime in on it.

And if Ginny wins, this nightmare will live on for the entire year of her reign.

I shake my head. The thought makes me ill. "I've got to get back up to the room. You two have fun. Be sure and let me know how it goes."

"No." Dad gives his head a firm shake. "Absolutely not. You're coming with us. No more hiding in your room."

"But . . ." I stammer.

But I'm not hiding.

But I can't be seen in the same room as Ginny.

Even if I could, I can't watch. I just can't.

"But nothing. We're going to go support your sister. All three of us." He takes me by the elbow and steers me toward the ballroom.

I'm in a panic.

Surely there's a way to wiggle my way out of this. But if there is, it's not coming to me. Each step we take fills me with dread. I can't speak. I can barely breathe. I feel like I'm being dragged to my own execution. Because if my presence in the audience outs Ginny, then it also outs me too.

I'm about to be publicly exposed as the liar that I am. In front of everyone. In front of Lisa and Torrie and all the other pageant girls who've been so nice to me.

In front of *Gray*.

"Ah, here it is," Susan says as we near the grand double doors leading to the ballroom.

It's happening. I'm about to be trapped between four walls with forty-nine beauty queens, six judges, and a sizable number of pageant officials who will all want to crucify me before all this is over.

Oh, and my twin.

Ginny will think I did it on purpose. She'll assume I marched down here of my own volition and showed my face in order to intentionally humiliate her and get her tossed out of the pageant. What else would she think after the horrible things I said to her earlier?

This is going to ruin our relationship. Things will never be the same between us. It will be one of those dire family events that linger . . . something we can't get past.

Kind of like the Adam situation, only worse. Much, much worse.

"Dad, I . . ." I search for some kind of excuse. There's got to be a ceremony of words that will stop this disaster in the making.

But it's too late. He's tucked my hand into the crook of his elbow, and we've already entered the room.

I bow my head and glue my gaze to my sneakers swallowing up the plush carpet. Maybe if I don't make eye contact with anyone, I'll stay invisible. After all, it's worked pretty well in the past.

Plus I definitely look different than I have all the other times I've been in this room. My face is scrubbed free of the makeup I wore last night. I didn't bother reapplying it because I'm no longer competing for the crown. I even managed to remove the hair extensions on my own.

If only I had my glasses to hide behind. But I don't. I've gotten so used to doing without them for the sake of vanity that I forgot to put them on after I shed my pageant persona and resumed life as myself.

"This looks like a good place to sit," I say, steering my dad toward three seats in the second-to-last row. If I leave it up to Susan, we'll be parked front row, center.

Luckily, Dad doesn't much care where we sit as long as we're here to witness Ginny in all her beauty queen glory.

We file in—first me, followed by Dad and finally Susan, situated in the aisle seat. I should have snagged the seat on the end. Then maybe after things got under way, I could have made my escape. But no. The only way I'm getting out of here is if I climb over both my parents.

Since that's clearly not an option, I sit as still as possible with my head ducked until the lights go dim.

"Welcome to the final day of the preliminary competition for Miss American Treasure!" the emcee booms.

The stage lights up like a Christmas tree, and I breathe a sigh of relief.

This is good. Every eye is glued to what's happening up there, and I'm just a nobody sitting in the dark. It's all going to be okay.

Safe now that the lights are out, I crane my neck for a glimpse of the judges' table. We're sitting straight across from it, on the far side of the room. I squint and right away I notice that something seems wrong.

Only five people are seated on the panel.

I squint harder, trying my best to determine who's missing. Then my stomach sinks, because I'm almost sure it's Gray.

What happened? Where is he?

I press a hand to my breastbone in an effort to calm my pounding heart. There's only one reason why Gray wouldn't be sitting alongside the other judges—we've been found out.

Someone must have seen us last night at the swan boats. But if that's the case, Ginny would have been expelled from the competition. I'm pretty sure spending the night with one of the judges is against the rules.

I lean closer to my dad and whisper in his ear. "Have you heard from Ginny lately?"

He answers without tearing his attention from the stage, where the emcee is thanking the long list of pageant sponsors. "I'm sure she's preoccupied at the moment, sweetheart."

"So that's a no, then?"

He shakes his head. "Pay attention. You'll get a chance to talk to her after the competition."

Or not. Because if she's been tossed out on her ear, she's probably upstairs burning all the books in my TBR pile.

Honestly, the odds of coming out of this week unscathed are diminishing by the second. How have I gotten myself into such a glittering, glamorous mess?

"Before we get started, I have a rather unusual announcement to make." The emcee's smile fades as she walks slowly toward the judges' table.

This is it.

"The Miss American Treasure family is sorry to say that one of our esteemed judges won't be joining us today . . ."

Oh God. I can't breathe. I think I'm going to faint.

"Mr. Gray Beckham has recused himself from the remainder of the competition. But we appreciate all he's done in support of Miss American Treasure and we're eager to welcome him back next year. Our involvement with his Miss Starlight pageant is one of the true highlights of our program, and we're honored to be in partnership with him. Please, everyone, let's all give Mr. Beckham a round of applause." She waves a hand toward the front row of the audience.

Gray stands, and the room bursts into applause.

I try my best to clap along, but I'm paralyzed. My body goes cold, and a terrible tremor courses through me.

Gray recused himself. Because of course he did. He's an honorable person, a gentleman. While I've been perfectly content to prance my way through the week, wreaking havoc and making a mockery out of the pageant regulations, he is intent on following the rules.

I admire him for it. I truly do. I just wish I could have been half that courageous.

If I could go back and relive the past few days, would I

do things differently? I like to think I would. I want to believe I'd never agree to impersonate my twin to begin with. Or that I would have told Gray the truth during our awkward, three-minute personal interview. At the very least, I wish I'd never lied to my dad and Susan.

But if I'm being honest with myself, I'm not entirely sure I wouldn't make the same choices. I was bound to tell Ginny the truth about Adam eventually. If I'd done so in the beginning, maybe I could have mitigated the damage and not made her feel as though it was all her fault.

My life was a mess of monotony before I came here. I can admit that now. And I think on some level, I needed to blow it up—to really destroy it and level it to the ground—before I could start over again and move on.

I take a deep breath, and my mind strays to Fire Safety Week at the library. I always bring a firefighter in to talk to the kids, and one of the things he says is that forest fires are dangerous, but like any bad thing, they can ultimately turn out for good.

Fire is nature's way of regenerating the woods and clearing the way for new growth. Some trees even depend on forest fires to spread their seed. The heat of the blaze causes pinecones to pop and explode, scattering seeds far and wide that have been waiting to germinate for years. As the land is being ravaged, it's already starting over. It's being reborn and rising from the ashes even before the flames burn away.

So every time I see a forest ablaze on television or pass a section of charred earth when I'm driving, I remember what it means: the forest is evolving. It's become stronger. The best is yet to come.

Is that true for me now? Will I walk away from the sky-high stilettos, the eyelash extensions, and the dazzling crown and be a better person?

I hope so. I want that with every last shred of my sorry heart.

Whether it happens or not, the damage is done. And in that moment, I know I will never kiss Gray Beckham again.

19

I sit, numb, as the contestants take the stage. They parade down the catwalk in a long, radiant row. And unlike the many, many pageants that Ginny has strong-armed me into watching during my lifetime, the faces of the girls competing for the crown are familiar to me.

I know these women. They lifted me up and encouraged me when I didn't think I'd be able to stand on my high heels without tumbling to the ground, much less strut down the runway with any level of confidence whatsoever. They squeezed my hands and wished me luck before I went onstage. They fed me cheeseburgers and celebrated my win in the talent competition with genuine hugs and well-wishes. Lisa Ng even tried to help me when it looked like Buttercup was having some kind of seizure.

I went into this charade assuming pageant girls were self-obsessed ditzes, but they're not. I'd fallen victim to a stereotype. These are accomplished, inspiring women—

women who cheered for me when it would have been so easy to cut me down so they could get ahead. But they didn't. Instead, they supported me, made sure I had my moment.

How did I repay them?

By lying to them and cheating, that's how.

God, I hate myself. Is there a single person in this room I haven't betrayed or disappointed in some way over the course of the past twenty-four hours? I squeeze my eyes closed. I know the answer to this question, and it makes me want to disappear.

For real this time.

I force my eyes back open so I can see Ginny. She's gorgeous, as always. Resplendent really, in that daring red dress. I can't help but wonder what she and Gray said to each other earlier in the hallway. Bile rises to the back of my throat with every possibility that flits through my mind.

I swallow it down as best I can.

"Are you okay?" my dad asks.

I nod. "Just peachy. Why do you ask?"

"Because you've got a death grip on my arm, sweetheart." He drops his gaze to my fingers, wrapped tightly around the tweed sleeve covering his bicep.

I hadn't realized I'd been touching my dad, much less acting as a human tourniquet. I bury my hands in my lap.

"Sorry. I guess I'm nervous." I give him a shaky smile. "For Ginny, obviously."

Yes, for Ginny.

But also for me.

Where do we go from here? Do my sister and I go back home to Texas and pretend none of this madness ever happened? Impossible. Things have changed between us in ways I still don't understand. Ginny will always be in my life. Obviously. But as I sit here in the dark, I can't imagine what our new relationship will look like. Or maybe I can, and I'm just not sure I like what I see.

Once the group of beauty queens has paraded up and down the stage, they disappear again behind the velvet curtain. The emcee calls each state winner to the stage, one at a time—in alphabetical order, as per usual—where the girls are presented with the box of questions. Miss Alabama, first out of the gate, draws a question about arming teachers as a response to the recent rise in school shootings.

If it were me up there, I'd know exactly what to say. As a school librarian, I have strong feelings about the subject. I can't see how adding more guns to the mix could possibly help matters, and I'm prepared to defend my opinion in a calm, rational manner.

But I'm no longer part of this pageant, so my opinion doesn't matter. Why do I keep forgetting that? And why, as we move through the alphabet onstage, do I keep answering the questions in my head as if I'm preparing for my turn?

This is Ginny's dream. Not yours.

Right. And when the emcee announces Miss Texas, I'm reminded why she's the family beauty queen and I'm the librarian.

My sister glows. There's no other way to describe it. Her skin is luminous, and her hair shimmers so much beneath the massive stage lamps that it looks as if she's been dipped in starlight. She's even somehow repaired the sash I cut in two. As for the dress, it's a knockout. It looks even better from a distance than it did up close. It's dramatic and theatrical— just the sort of thing a newly crowned Miss American Treasure would wear on her victory walk.

As gorgeous as she looks, it's not her appearance that makes her look so regal. It's her confidence.

Ginny carries herself like a queen.

It's the one thing we don't have in common. We've got the same DNA, the same family, and most of the same formative life experiences. We grew up in the same home and went to the same schools. When we look in the mirror, we see the same, identical face. But I've never had even a fraction of Ginny's belief in herself.

It's something I'm going to work on from here on out. Because Adam never could have broken my heart if I hadn't let him. If only I'd believed in myself a little more, his obsession with Ginny wouldn't have crushed me the way it had. Of course I would have been devastated. But maybe I wouldn't have held on to the pain for so long. Maybe I wouldn't have blamed my sister.

If only.

"Miss Texas, please select your question." The emcee waits as Ginny chooses a folded square of paper from the acrylic box in the reigning Miss American Treasure's arms.

An eerie calm washes over me. It doesn't matter what's written on that slip of paper. Ginny lives for this kind of thing. She'll answer her question with eloquence and grace. If she can defend *Fifty Shades of Grey* as a piece of high literature, she can do anything. And I know better than anyone just how adept she is at the art of persuasion. I still have the spray tan and blisters on my feet to prove it.

The emcee unfolds the piece of paper. "Are you ready, Miss Texas?"

Ginny flashes her best beauty queen smile. "Yes, ma'am."

"Very good. Once I've read your question, you'll have two minutes to answer." The emcee clears her throat. "Here's your question: What family member has had the biggest influence on your life and why?"

Perfect.

I know exactly what Ginny's response will be. In fact, I've heard her practice answer for this very question, and it's quite moving.

She's going to talk about our mother. She's going to mention our mother's illness and the effect her death had on Ginny's life when she was a little girl, and then she'll conclude by saying her quest to become Miss American Treasure is her way of honoring our mom and keeping her memory alive. By the time her two minutes are up, there won't be a dry eye in the house.

I sit back in my chair and wait for the waterworks.

But then something strange happens. Ginny doesn't mention our mother. She doesn't say anything at all. For several long seconds, she just stands there, wide-eyed, quietly staring out into the audience.

My dad, Susan, and I all exchange glances. What's happening? We've never seen Ginny freeze like this. I have the sudden urge to leap out of my chair, dive onstage, and answer the question for her.

Wouldn't that be a perfect spectacle?

Not necessary, though, because somewhere around the thirty second-mark, Ginny clears her throat and finally starts talking.

"Up until today, I thought I knew the answer to this question. I've always considered my mother, Miss American Treasure 1975, to be the most influential person in my life. But something happened this afternoon that made me realize that's not true." Ginny's gaze sweeps the crowd, searching, until it lands on me.

My mouth goes dry.

She holds my gaze as she continues. "Most of the people in this room don't know this, but I'm an identical twin. My sister, Charlotte, is only two minutes older than I am, but she's been a role model for me since the day we were born."

What is she doing?

All around me, heads are swiveling my direction. Somewhere near the front of the room, I hear a gasp.

No. I shake my head. *Don't do it, Ginny.*

But she's made her choice, and even when the timer dings, indicating her two minutes are up, she refuses to give up the microphone and keeps right on talking.

"My twin is smarter than I am. She's kinder and more compassionate. She's loves books and children and she's been so sweet to my dog this week that Buttercup is going home with her instead of with me. Charlotte is exactly the kind of person I want to be when I grow up."

A sob racks my body. I am shaking so violently that my teeth are chattering.

"I've done an appalling thing," Ginny says, and her voice breaks. Something deep inside me breaks along with it. "All week, I've asked my twin to pretend to be me. I had an allergic reaction and couldn't compete, so I asked Charlotte to take my place until I could get better. I dressed her up like me and taught her to walk, talk, and think like me. I asked her to cheat for me, and I had no idea what a terrible toll it would take on her."

The room is buzzing now. It hums with the fury of a thousand bees. At the far end of the runway, the pageant director is climbing onto the stage.

"In conclusion, I just want to say I'm sorry." Ginny takes a deep breath. "To all my fellow contestants, the Miss American Treasure organization, and to my parents. But most of all, to Charlotte. I should have been the one emulating *you* instead of the other way around. Please forgive me."

My sister offers the microphone back to the emcee, who looks beyond shell-shocked, but then she snatches it back to add one more thing. "Oh, and I quit. I officially withdraw from the rest of this pageant."

And just like that, Ginny's dream dies a painful, public death.

The scene in the ballroom is chaotic.

The last six contestants don't get a chance to answer their onstage questions, nor are the top twenty finalists announced. The pageant comes to a screeching halt as everyone tries to make sense of what's just happened.

The pageant director looks as if she's on the verge of a

heart attack and I have to be honest, Dad looks pretty furious himself. I want to stay and apologize to him and Susan. Eventually, I will.

But first, I need to get to Ginny.

I can't believe what she just did. She sacrificed herself for me. She didn't have to do it. We could have worked things out. She could have waited until the pageant was over, and we could have talked it through.

She'll never have a chance at the title again. After a lifetime of pursuing the crown, Ginny will never be Miss American Treasure.

This seems unfathomable to me, and yet, when I finally push past the agitated mob of people and reach my twin, she doesn't look at all like a person whose dream has just withered and died. Her lips are curved into a serene smile, and she holds her head high. As always, she looks like royalty.

I throw my arms around her with such force that we both nearly topple to the ground.

"You're crazy, you know that?" I whisper into her mass of hair extensions.

"It was all true," she says. "Every word. I'm just sorry it took me so long to tell you how amazing you are. I guess I thought you knew."

I sniff. Loudly. My God, I don't remember the last time I cried this hard. "Nope."

She pulls back to look me in the eyes. "Well, you are. Adam is a disgusting pig. And I haven't exactly been the nicest person to be around lately either. I went a little crown crazy."

"It's okay." I smile. "We're even now."

And for a wacky, wonderful moment, everything seems okay. All around us, people are yelling or crying or cursing, but in our little bubble, life is good. It's just Ginny and me, and for the first time since childhood, we're one. The broken cord that once held us together so tightly is intact again.

But then my gaze drifts over her shoulder and I see Gray.

Our eyes meet, and I want to go to him and apologize. I want to tell him that even though I've acted like a phony and a fake, my feelings for him are genuine. I've fallen for him, and that's a fact.

But there's too much fiction between us.

When I take a step toward him, his beautiful blue eyes go cold. And then he turns his back on me and leaves without saying a word as I choke on a sob.

"Charlotte, what's wrong?" Ginny says. She follows my gaze until her attention lands squarely on Gray's slumped shoulders.

After everything we've been through this week, I still haven't opened up to her about Gray. I'm still holding on to to one last secret.

No more.

I take a deep, shuddering breath.

No more pretending.

No more lies.

"I have so much to tell you," I say. Then I reach for my twin, and hand in hand, we walk out of the ballroom and leave the Miss American Treasure pageant behind.

Once and for all.

20

It takes nearly a month for my faux tan to fade away.

Seriously, what kind of chemicals must they put in that stuff? It can't be healthy. Not that it matters much to me personally, since I'll never be using self-tanner again. Ever.

But the gradual transition of my skin back to its standard shade—a color I lovingly refer to as bibliophile pale—is as good a way as any to mark the time. A lot has happened.

A whole lot.

For starters, after all the drama that concluded the Miss American Treasure prelims, the Gormans promptly pulled an Elvis and left the building. It was a tense ride to the airport, considering Dad and Susan were still barely speaking to both Ginny and me. If we'd been a decade or two younger, we'd have been grounded for life. Alas, we're pushing thirty. Ginny and I each wrote handwritten letters of apology to all forty-nine of the other pageant contestants, but that was our choice. The only punishment our parents have enforced is a weekly Sunday-night dinner where we're regularly encouraged to talk about our feelings so that our family never has a repeat of the pageant debacle ever again.

It's not so bad, really. For starters, Susan is an amazing chef. Ginny and I are both convinced that the family dinner thing was her idea, because it gives her a chance to channel her inner Julia Child on a regular basis. Over dishes like boeuf bourguignon, quiche Lorraine, and paper-thin crêpes, I've learned a lot about my twin.

It's crazy. Before the pageant, I could have sworn I knew everything there was to know about Ginny, her deep appreciation for the Fifty Shades trilogy notwithstanding. I'm still not over that, by the way. I'll *never* be over it.

But there are other things—things that make me realize she hasn't just been floating lazily through her adult life on a wave of duck-face selfies and #outfitoftheday posts on Instagram. She's been saving money. Piles of it. I always knew she made a decent living off her sponsored social media posts, but that was just the tip of the iceberg. All those tiaras she so proudly displays on the shelves of her upscale apartment in Dallas's trendy Bishop Arts District are worth far more than their weight in rhinestones.

Each of Ginny's pageant wins has brought in some serious cash. As it turns out, she was telling the truth—most beauty pageants are, in fact, *scholarship competitions*. *Miss Congeniality* is more of a documentary than a rom-com. Throughout her lifetime as a beauty queen, my sister has accumulated almost $200,000 in money earmarked for higher education.

Even more surprising, she's planning on using every dime. Now that she's aged out of the Miss American Treasure program, she's begun filling out applications for textile and art programs all over the country. Her ultimate goal is to attend the Parsons School of Design in New York City. I'm fully convinced she'll end up on *Project Runway* at some point. If anyone can "make it work" Tim Gunn–style and handle the intense pressure of reality television, it's my twin.

In the meantime, she's still taking twirling lessons and competing in the pageants that have divisions for contestants who've passed the big 3-0.

Crazy, right? I would have assumed that if anything could get a person blackballed from the pageant circuit, it would be having your identical twin take your place after you've suffered an allergy attack instead of withdrawing from the competition altogether. But no. Apparently, her onstage confession is being seen as a sign of personal growth. Ginny is even using the whole experience as something to talk about in her personal interviews.

Some things never change.

Then again, some things do.

Ginny isn't the only one who has new career aspirations. I do too.

I still love being a librarian. Books are my heart and soul. They've been there for me all my life—in good times and bad. Case in point: I've reread *Pride and Prejudice* five times since I left Orlando. I know that sounds nuts, but something about disappearing into the pages of my favorite comfort read helps me forget the less than spectacular moments of late, while at the same time allowing me to savor the moments I spent with Gray . . .

My own personal Mr. Darcy.

For a few days, at least.

I wonder what he'd think if he knew I'd decided to take my passion for literature one step further by writing a book. I've only got fifty pages so far, but it's a start. Every night after work, I sit down at my laptop and try my best to put what happened at the Miss American Treasure pageant into words. It's quite a story. I've no idea if it will ever get published or if anyone out there really wants to read about a girl who lost her mind a little bit and compromised everything she believed in, all in pursuit of a crown made of paste and plastic. But it's about more than that, really. It's about what it truly means to be beautiful, inside and out. And that's a lesson I'm still learning. I'm not sure I'll ever fully grasp it, but I'm trying.

In any case, writing about my tenure as an accidental beauty queen helps me make sense of the things I did and the choices I made. I just wish things could have turned out differently for Gray and me.

The Miss Starlight pageant took place two weeks after Lisa Ng was crowned Miss American Treasure. I wanted to be there. I wanted to see the amazing way Gray honors the memory of his sister, up close and personal. I even went so far as to check out flights to Boston, where the pageant takes place every year. My credit card was right there beside my laptop, but I just couldn't do it.

Every time my cursor hovered over the purchase button, I remembered the look on his face when our eyes met in the ballroom after Ginny's onstage confession. I remembered the sag in his shoulders when he turned his back and walked away. I remembered the way his silence slayed me with deadly precision in a way that sharp words would have never been able to achieve.

I'd wanted him to tell me what I'd done was wrong. I'd wanted him to take all his brooding hostility and unleash it at me in a torrent of blame and admonition. Because then I would have known that what we'd shared had been real, that it had meant as much to him as it did to me.

Maybe it didn't. Deep down, I suspect it did. But thinking and knowing are two different things, and even if Gray had fallen for me in the same way I'd fallen for him, I still wasn't sure he'd forgiven me. I couldn't just show up at his pageant and ruin one of the most meaningful days of his life.

Instead, I stayed home and used my credit card to make an anonymous donation to the Miss Starlight foundation. My contribution was enough to pay for five large tiaras for girls in Gray's program. I've been waiting for photos from the event to show up on social media, but so far I've only seen a handful on the Boston local news sites. I can't rely on Ginny to keep me updated, because in the biggest shocker of all, she's completely deleted her online presence.

So here I sit, balanced in one of the tiny student workstations in the library after school, scrolling through posts bearing the Miss Starlight hashtag while Buttercup snores in my lap.

Before the school year started, I collected every bit of data I could find on the benefits of reading-assistance dogs. Apparently, children feel more comfortable reading aloud to pups than they do in a traditional classroom setting. It's no wonder—dogs are patient and nonjudgmental. They lavish praise on readers in the form of tail wags and puppy kisses regardless of whether every word was pronounced correctly. As a result, kids read more. And everyone knows practice makes perfect.

After I presented the evidence to the school principal, he agreed to let me bring Buttercup to school with me twice a week and set up a quiet reading area in the corner of the library closest to my desk, so I could keep tabs on things. So far, the program has been a huge hit. Buttercup hasn't been officially certified as a reading-assistance dog yet, but she seems to be a natural. The kids especially love the way her big ears swivel to and fro when they tell her a story.

At the moment, she's exhausted. Her little paws twitch in her sleep, and I wonder if she's chasing Crookshanks the cat in her dreams. Because yes, the Harry Potter series is a big favorite in my library.

I scroll through the most recent posts about the pageant, and suddenly, Buttercup lifts her head. Her big eyes open wide, and her ears prick forward like they always do when she's on high alert for the UPS man.

I rest my hand on her back. "Calm down. We're the only ones here at this hour, besides the janitor. And you love him. He carries dog biscuits in his pockets."

"Shall I come back when I'm properly armed with Milk-Bones, then?" someone behind me says.

Not just *any* someone.

I know that voice. I know it well. It's deep and languorous. So velvety smooth that I feel it as much as I hear it. I love it best when it's reciting lines from Austen or Shakespeare. Even better, when it calls me Hermione.

But as much as I love that honeyed voice, as much as

I've longed to hear it whisper my real name, it belongs to a man who lives in another state. A man who may very well despise me.

Buttercup hops down from my lap and scurries out of view. I know I should follow, but I'm afraid to look. What if it's only wishful thinking? What if I've spent so much time thinking about Gray that I've started hearing things? If that's the case, I won't be able to bear the crushing disappointment of turning around and finding an empty space where I hope and pray my favorite pageant judge is standing right now.

Take a chance.

I swallow. How many times have I wished I'd had the courage to do the right thing in Orlando? *Countless* times. I can't go back, but I can do the courageous thing now. I have to. After all, isn't that what Lizzie Bennet and Jo March would do?

I rise from the tiny chair and turn around. Sure enough, this isn't a fantasy or some kind of alternate universe. He's here . . . in my library, filling up the space as only a man of Darcyesque proportions could.

"Gray." His name is only one syllable, but my voice breaks, turning it into two.

"Hermione," he says, and his smile is bittersweet.

I'm tempted to smile back and let myself believe that his use of the familiar nickname, coupled with the fact that he's *here*, means I'm forgiven. Or better yet, that he's been thinking about me as much as I've been thinking about him. But I don't, because I'm keenly aware that he might only be calling me by my wizard name because I've never told him my real one.

"It's Charlotte, actually." I bite down hard on my bottom lip, because there's a sob rising up from somewhere deep inside me and I'm afraid if I let down my guard for even a second, it will come pouring out of me in a display of raw emotion that will send Gray running back to Boston before he's had a chance to tell me why he's here.

But then I give up the fight. I've been pretending for far too long.

"So I guess my Accio spell worked," I say as tears stream down my face. "Here you are."

It's my lame attempt at a joke, but make no mistake—if I'd thought for a minute that a summoning spell would have gotten him here any sooner, I'd have given my wand a serious workout.

I hold my breath as he closes the distance between us. Then before I can process what's happening, his arms are around me and my damp face is pressed against the smooth wool of his suit jacket.

He presses a tender kiss to the top of my head. "Don't cry, love. Please don't cry."

Love.

As nicknames go, it's my favorite. I like it even better than Hermione.

I lift my face and my gaze collides with his. My breath catches in my throat, just like it did when I stood before him in a pretty pink gown before he knew my name. Still, he saw me. Somehow those sapphire eyes always have.

"How did you know where to find me?" What stroke of fate brought him to my library? Because I definitely wasn't forthcoming with my work address during any of our pageant interludes.

"Your twin. She wrote to me. Didn't she tell you?"

I shake my head. I'm too moved to attempt speaking.

Ginny wrote Gray a letter?

He shrugs a single, muscular shoulder. "She said it was her fault that you lied, and if I didn't get down here and sweep you off your feet as soon as possible, she was going to come up to Boston and drag me back to Texas with her."

Wow.

Okay, then.

I'm now indebted to my sister. Big-time. Because at last I have a chance to apologize to Gray in person.

"I'm sorry. So very, very sorry." I swallow. "About everything."

He brushes a tear from my cheek with the pad of his thumb. "It's okay. I knew something was . . . off. I just didn't know what it was. I'll admit I was surprised. Stunned might be a more accurate description. But then I got back to Boston, away from all the pageant hoopla, and I realized you'd tried to tell me. More than once, as I recall."

He's going easy on me, and I'm glad. I really am, but still. "I could have tried harder."

He lets out a soft laugh that I feel deep in the center of my being. "We both could have done things differently. I assure you, I don't make a habit out of falling in love with pageant contestants. I'm no angel, Hermione. I should have recused myself the minute you sat down at my table during the personal interviews."

Did Gray Beckham just tell me he loves me?

He did.

But he's not finished. He takes my chin between his thumb and forefinger and holds my face still so that I'm forced to look deep into his eyes. "I knew it wasn't you, you know."

I feel my brow crinkle. I'm not sure what he's talking about. "What? When?"

"The morning after we made love." He pauses to smile, and my cheeks go hot. "I was on the way to meet with the Miss American Treasure director and tell her I couldn't continue to judge the pageant, and I ran into a woman in a long red dress."

Ginny in the Jessica Rabbit dress.

I nod. I know the exact moment he's referring to now,

because I was there. For just a split second, and then I'd run. I couldn't stand watching him look at Ginny the way he always looked at me.

It's not until his words sink in that I realize he hadn't. He'd barely looked at her at all.

I knew it wasn't you, you know.

"She looked like you. A lot like you—I'll admit—and she had the Miss Texas sash draped across her gown. But somehow I knew. I looked into her eyes, and I didn't find you there. It didn't make sense at the time, but I knew it wasn't my Hermione." His voice goes rough. Insistent. Maybe it's the ache in his tone or maybe it's knowing that he's the only one in Orlando who could tell me apart from my twin sister, but I feel something stir deep inside me. It's the healing of old wounds. "I need you to know that."

I nod and try to smile, but my chin goes all wobbly again.

I don't want to cry anymore. How can I not, though? And what do you say to a person who recognized you at a time when even your own family couldn't see you clearly?

I have no idea. I'm at a loss.

For as long as I can remember, I've been a lover of words. But I can't find the ones to properly express my feelings for this man. None of them seem adequate. Not even *love*.

But I whisper that one to him anyway, just so he knows. "I'm in love with you, Gray."

And then—in a place as far away as possible from the

glitz and glam of pageant life, surrounded by row upon row of hardbound books and the sweet perfume of literature and longing—Charlotte Gorman kisses Gray Beckham.

It feels wonderful and new, like a very first kiss. And in a way, I suppose it is. But I know with every beautiful beat of my heart that it won't be our last.

Our story is just beginning.

acknowledgments

This book goes out with heartfelt gratitude and love to my family and friends. I also want to extend special thanks to my wonderful agent, Elizabeth Winick Rubinstein, my fabulous editor, Marla Daniels, and the entire team at Gallery Books. I am also indebted to Ashley Martinez and Stephi Williams for inviting me to judge the Miss United States pageant last year. I obviously had the time of my life.